THE LAST YEAR OF THE WILD

THE LAST YEAR

OF THE

WILD

VOLUME 1
WINTER

LIZZIE PEPPER

ILLUSTRATIONS BY GRACE MORAN

Troubador Publishing Ltd
Unit E2 Airfield Business Park,
Harrison Road, Market Harborough,
Leicestershire. LE16 7UL
Tel: 0116 2792299
Email: books@troubador.co.uk
Web: www.troubador.co.uk/matador

ISBN 978 1 80313 639 4

British Library Cataloguing in Publication Data.
A catalogue record for this book is available from the British Library.

Printed and bound in Great Britain by 4edge Limited
Typeset in 11pt Minion Pro by Troubador Publishing Ltd, Leicester, UK

Matador is an imprint of Troubador Publishing Ltd

CONTENTS

THE LAST YEAR OF THE WILD

MEET THE CAST...

In order of appearance:

Rufus
Species: **Robin**
Scientific name: *Erithacus rubecula*
His mission - To defend the Human
'Beings' and protect his community.

Captain Mallard
Species: **Mallard Duck**
Scientific name: *Anas platyrhynchos*
His mission – To help Commander
Bewick and to captain the Starling
Regiment.

Percy
Species: **Woodpigeon**
Scientific name: *Columba palumbus*
His mission – To deliver the Royal Messenger Service.

Skyla
Species: **Robin**
Scientific name: *Erithacus rubecula*
Her mission – To make sure Rufus's community stays alive whilst he is away.

Commander Bewick
Species: **Bewick Swan**
Scientific name: *Cygnus columbianus bewickii*
His mission – To defend the Northern Territories.

Contents

Corax
Species: **Cormorant**
Scientific name: *Phalacrocorax carbo*
His mission – To take over the Northern Territories.

Jack Sparrow
Species: **House Sparrow**
Scientific name: *Passer domesticus*
His mission – To find his family, keep up with Rufus and stay alive.

Northern England

PRELUDE

'This Robin is barely alive and the Sparrow feels lifeless. There must be something you can do for them? I just couldn't leave them behind, the poor birds are smothered in the oil,' a young man shouted in exasperation, as he raced to pull a large wooden rescue crate out of the back of his van, battling against the high winds and heavy rain.

'Jake, how many times do I need to tell you? We've no space left for any more,' a flustered man replied from the doorway of a Coastguard Centre, which stood high on a cliff edge, overlooking an angry swirling North Sea.

Jake carefully set the crate down in the doorway and assessed the skies above.

'No, we must keep going. You've just got to make more space inside. I don't care how you do it but I am not stopping now. Not until we have helped every single bird.'

'You're crazy. It is far too dangerous in this storm, come on inside,' the man demanded, watching Jake running back to his van, leaving him with the dying birds curled up in the crate beside him as he did so.

Seconds later, his wheels splashed through a deep puddle as he accelerated out of the car-park. As the van's engine roared off into the distance, a gust of wind swept through, causing a makeshift sign dangling above the Centre's doorway to creak loudly. Roughly written were the words…

CHAPTER 1

TRAPPED

A little later, deep inside the Coastguard Centre, trapped within the confines of his rescue crate, Rufus the Robin was desperately trying to escape as he listened to the unfamiliar noises in the darkness around him. Bang, crash…

'What…what was that?' he shouted out loud in his soft Scottish accent, pausing for a moment to listen intently, before continuing, 'Who's there?'

Seconds later…a snapping noise and another bang sounded.

'Is that you Skyla…? Hey. Can anyone hear me?' Rufus called. 'If I could just see, this would be whole lot easier.'

Straining against the black goo that held his eye lids firmly shut, he tried to ignore the waves of panic racing through his tiny brown feathered body and small red chest.

'Grrrrr…,' he growled, hoping to defend himself from any danger which might be lurking nearby.

Clamping his beak together, he strained to open his eyes, eventually collapsing on the hard floor of his crate with exhaustion. Feeling trapped, blinded by darkness, his eyes stung with pain. His only option was to lay still and play dead.

'Where am I…?' he whispered to himself.

Suddenly, the crate shook beneath him and a loud crash sounded again, followed by the familiar smell of a 'Being' wafting past his nostrils.

'I have got to get out of here,' he exclaimed, determined to move his limp and heavy body.

Stirring up all the energy he had left, Rufus's patience broke as he shouted angrily at himself, 'Just…open will you.'

Amazingly, it worked as he managed to force open his eyelids, allowing him enough time to focus on the human's face, which was staring directly back at him. For a few seconds Rufus remained motionless, realising that he had never been this close to a 'Being' before. How odd it looked he thought? Standing upright, with oversized eyes and strange useless looking feathers growing out of the top if its head. And, what kind of food could they eat with that shape of beak, he wondered? Puzzling as it was, Rufus couldn't contain his urge to escape.

'Arrh. Beings,' he screamed, dragging himself across the floor of his crate as best he could to get out of the way. 'Just don't…touch me, it feels too weird.'

His eyes slammed shut again, causing him to wobble, tripping as he did so over what felt like a warm and feathery ball. Another bird maybe? he thought.

There was no time to check, as he heard to his horror the sound of more Beings' feet heading in his direction, chirping in their high-pitched squeaky voices as they got closer.

'Mo, you have to put…one to sleep…and quickly,' Rufus roughly translated, only understanding a few words.

Blindly, Rufus helplessly listened to the chaos around him, as the swish of the Beings' clothes wafted their suffocating chemical smell in his direction again.

"Stand back," he heard them cry, as he tightly curled his body up hoping that by some miracle he might actually be able to hide from them.

'Now…do it now,' one Being squeaked in the commotion.

'No,' Rufus screamed, defending himself and wishing they could understand him. 'No, wait. I need to get back to my garden, they all need me. I am Rufus…Rufus Robin of 42…Barton Gardens….'

The sharp pain of the needle entered Rufus's brown feathered back, instantly immobilising his whole body. Petrified, he quickly lost the ability to speak and smell. As his hearing disappeared, darkness flooded through his body, plunging him into a deep sleep.

CHAPTER 2

NIGHTFALL

Further inland the storm had run out of energy, as dusk turned to nightfall around the sides of an icy dark lake in the North East of England. The atmosphere was almost still, only occasionally interrupted by the sound of twittering birds wriggling to keep warm amongst the deep stiff grasses surrounding the lake.

In a muddy patch by the water's edge, the peaceful scene was broken by the sound of flapping wings from the skies above, swishing as they came into land.

'Captain Mallard, do you have a moment? May I have your permission to speak freely?' a military voice whispered in the darkness.

After a few seconds, a rather exasperated reply came, 'Yes, what is it now, Starling Officer 167?'

'Sir, I feel we should go and investigate the emergency message we received earlier. What if it is for real and Corax's Army has struck again?'

'May I remind you Officer, you are trained to think and not feel, is that clear?' Captain Mallard sighed and then continued, 'The call sounded like a hoax to me. A deadly black sea? Never have I heard of such a thing?'

'Sir, the message said hundreds of birds have died,' the Starling informed tentatively.

'I doubt that, there's hardly a hundred of us left to die,' the Captain replied sarcastically. 'We already have enough to worry about right now without this. Can't you feel the rain is about to start again? Honestly, there'll be flooding everywhere and still no food for us all.'

Fumbling with his feathers uneasily, the Starling Officer tried one last time.

'The coast isn't far, it might be worth checking it. I mean, what if Corax is not content with just taking over our lands but wishes to take over the ocean as well?'

After a few short seconds of silence, the Officer watched the silhouette of the Captain plodding around thoughtfully. The young Officer began to wonder if he had overstepped the mark?

'Fine, go,' the Captain finally announced. 'But fly fast. Nightfall is here and I do not wish to be interrogated by the Nightshift as to why you're out well after the safety of the daylight hours. And, if I am right and this is some ridiculous hoax, I want the culprit caught. Do I make myself clear?'

'Yes, Sir. Thank you, Sir,' answered the Officer mechanically.

'Good, go quickly. Oh, and Officer, for your information,

I hear that Rufus Robin is also missing, not that it surprises me. You know, the Scottish one,' the Captain added. 'Try and find him, will you? The last thing we need is a fresh fight over his abandoned garden territory at this time of night.'

'Sir, you have my word. We will do all we can,' the Officer confirmed with an eager voice, accompanied by the sound of his rustling feathers as he flew up into the darkening sky to gather his squadron.

For a moment the only sound which followed was that of the Mallard Captain's slow breathing in the chilly night air. A few seconds later the noise of squelching and the rustling of the reeds being pushed out of the way could be heard, as the Captain wearily returned to his roost for the cold night ahead.

CHAPTER 3

THE
DISASTER ZONE

'This is definitely not a hoax,' the Starling Officer in Charge wearily expressed a little while later. As he and his fellow Officers from the Regiment watched in horror, as large lumps of poisonous stinking black goo bubbled out of the ocean. Each one moving slowly up the once golden beach, suffocating any form of life in its path.

'Come on we must try and save as many as we can,' said one Junior Starling, not quite believing the scene in front of him.

Perched high on the cliff top, the Regiment of Starlings scanned the swirling black sea in front of them for any sign of life. In the distance, bright lights shone from an enormous ship, which was partly submerged. Its steel frame groaned against the choppy waters, as though they were trying to swallow it whole.

With several rescue boats already on the scene, the ship's passengers' screams cut through the night air. The atmosphere suddenly intensified, as the Starlings watched the Beings slowly appeared to be losing their ability to breathe.

'No, stop. It looks too dangerous, probably poisonous. If we get too close, we could die amongst them,' shouted the Starling Officer in Charge at the front of the line.

Terrified at the scene which was unfolding in front of them and unable to comprehend their next move, the Starlings stood motionless. Flinching, every time the black lumps managed to strangle any form of life and looking with uncertainty towards their 'Officer in Charge,' as to what the next command might be? It wasn't long before the smell of fumes started to fill their nostrils. Coughing, they were quickly aware that their speckled green, purple and brown feathers had begun to feel heavy, as the fumes felt like they were actually sticking to their wings.

Taking the Starlings by surprise, a helicopter appeared as it thundered through the night sky, its lights flooding the entire scene, the deafening noise dominating the landscape.

'Sir, what do we do now?' the Junior Starling shouted.

'There's nothing we can do,' the Officer in Charge replied, trying to peck the goo out of his feathers, 'we must head back.'

'Wait. Look down there, is that Corax's Army?' the

Junior Starling shouted, noticing a flock of rather smug looking dark Rooks landing close by, he quickly decided. 'So, they caused this as well? We can't stand by and just watch this happen. Come on!'

'No, remain in line,' shouted the Officer in Charge, 'you are right though, they do look guilty. It is far too risky for us to approach them now and by the looks of it we are completely outnumbered.' He sighed deep in thought and then announced slowly, 'Corax must be stopped but we cannot do this alone. Come on, we must get back to the Station to strengthen our guard and let Captain Mallard know what has happened.'

'What about the young Robin that's missing, Rufus isn't it?' questioned the Junior Starling, remembering that they were supposed to be searching for a lost Leader.

'We will do one last fly by and search for him,' the Officer in Charge instructed. 'Be careful though, stay close together and away from the fumes. Take a deep breath before you take to the wing, do you all understand me?'

Together they nodded and edged forward, feeling the slippery solid rock beneath them. As the wind started gently to lift their wings, each one took a deep breath and stepped over the edge, taking flight.

Straight away, they felt the weight of their bodies plummeting down, the wind screaming past their ears, their hearts racing, as the black slimy sea raced closer and closer to them as they fell. One by one, they began to unfold their frozen wings, feeling the blood pouring into each feathered finger. Powered by the wind, they rode over the blackened sea searching the area for any sign of Rufus. As they did so, the Rooks of Corax's Army watched them flying above whilst they stood guard to protect the disaster, which they appeared so proud of.

Silently flying in formation, the Starlings swirled in the night air, turning towards what was left of the beach. As they scanned the area, they noticed the large hunched shapes of Beings gathered on the beach, calling out against the winter winds and coughing furiously. On closer inspection, they appeared to be pulling what looked like the remains of birds barely hanging onto life from the clutches of the goo, carefully placing them on trays of different sizes. To their horror, the Starlings watched as the trays were carried away, to be hidden from view.

The Starling Officer in Charge shouted above the winds. 'We can't save them now, they're in the hands of the Beings. There is no hope for them.'

With heavy hearts, the flock carried on flying as fast as they dare, feeling increasingly vulnerable that Corax's Army were watching their every move.

'Let's make for home as we can barely breathe. On my command, bank to the left.'

The whole flock followed in tight unison, and as they did so the Officer in Charge turned for one last time to look at scene below him. A feeling of hopelessness flooded his body, as he wondered if there could have been more he might have done? Yet, as he noticed the deep look of satisfaction within the eyes of the Rooks below, their glares sent shivers through him, energising his flight home.

* * *

In complete darkness, deep within the confines of his rescue crate, Rufus was trying to work out whether he was actually alive or dead.

As he emerged from his deep sleep, it was only the feel of his racing heart that reassured him. Moments later, his hearing began to return and he was aware of weird sounds whirling around him.

The smells wafting up his nostrils felt instantly uncomfortable. Rarely had he smelt anything before, yet the stench of the Beings was unbearable, putrid and chemical. Especially as he couldn't move away from it, his whole body still feeling heavy, unmoveable.

Click, bang, rustle.

'Who's there? I am Rufus, back off…,' he snarled.

Seconds later, he felt the excruciating pain of the Beings hands folding tightly around his useless body.

CHAPTER 4

THE GARDEN TERRITORY

'Good morning, 42 Barton Gardens, this is Percy from your local North East branch of the Royal Pigeon Messenger Service speaking,' announced Percy, using one tone of voice only. 'Please be alert, Pearla the cat is on the prowl again.'

Looking happy with himself, the rather overweight silvery Wood Pigeon with a light lilac chest, perched on the damp branches of an old Pine Tree that grew in the middle of an ordinary looking cul-de-sac of houses.

As a weak sun signalled a new day, Percy listened as the other Messenger Pigeons in the distance also delivered their morning calls, in the same and rather flat tone with which Percy had sung.

Realising, much to his dismay, that his own Community had not responded, he rearranged his feathers, protruded his chest and began to repeat his toneless message…' 'Good morning, 42 Barton Gardens, this is Percy from your local North East branch of the Royal Pigeon service. Please be alert, Pearla the cat is…'

"On the prowl,"…yes, Percy. We heard you the first time,' began a rather stroppy voice from within a spindly bush close by.

On closer inspection, Percy noticed that snuggled up within the bush were a pair of brightly coloured Chaffinch Songbirds who looked extremely unhappy at being woken up so early.

'That flipping cat is always on the prowl, it is nothing new. In fact, that ginger cat is so fat I would be amazed if she managed to catch a mouse, never mind us lot!' sniggered the male Chaffinch, fluffing up his pinkish chest and rearranging the white and black flight feathers on his back to generate heat. 'Do you have anything actually useful to tell us Percy?'

Percy, who prided himself on delivering a professional service, shook his feathers and neatly repositioned them and then arched his neck in self-importance.

'Indeed, I have. Your weather forecast for today is as follows,' he announced looking to up to the sky to read the clouds. 'Arrh…I see rather dark cumulus congestus clouds, which appear to be gathering together…'

'In English please,' interrupted one of the Chaffinches.

'Rain, rain. It's going to rain and for quite some time,' Percy finished in exasperation.

'Are you sure? Rain again? We may as well live on the sea. This place will go under water soon, unless it stops raining.'

As Percy began to defend his weather forecast for the day, the rumble of hunger in the tummies of the Chaffinches quickly changed their mood.

'I am starving,' complained the female Chaffinch perched beside her partner, flexing her, lighter brown feathers ready for flight.

'And where exactly do you suppose we will find food? Everything is soggy, damp, and tell me… where are all the bugs these days?' the male Chaffinch asked beside her.

'Bugs? Who needs bugs? You wait 'they' will fill that table in no time,' she replied, nodding to the Being's house at the bottom of the garden.

'You're living in hope, aren't you? It was mid-day yesterday before they fed us and even then, it was nuts. Just the same old nuts. I'd like to see them survive on nuts,' he replied grumbling and then turning to Percy questioned. 'Honestly, if our Robin Leader was here he'd have something to say about this, don't you think Percy? Come to think of it, where is young Rufus? It is so odd for a Robin to have abandoned his position. His father would have had something to say about that I am sure. Mind you, he had better turn up quickly, or there'll be a huge fight over this garden territory.'

'Oh, there's nothing like a good Robin fight if you ask me,' chuckled the female Chaffinch, nudging her partner as she did so and turning to involve Percy. 'Don't you think so?'

'May I suggest, that it is the very last thing we need.

Robin wars never end well. Anyway, Rufus will return I am sure. He has never left his territory before,' expressed Percy, distracted by the angry look which Pearla was directing at him for having messed up any chance of bird breakfast. Curling her bushy tail high in disgust, as cats do, she headed back towards the Beings house.

Instantly, feeling happy that his task was completed, Percy flew optimistically towards the bird table, also having felt his tummy rumble.

* * *

As Percy landed, he was quickly joined by a Blackbird, arching his black tail feathers as he hopped towards him. His beak was light orange, the same colour as the lines around his black beady eyes, which wore an expression of concern. Percy instantly recognised him, so he gathered himself up for a tough conversation, stretching out his chest with authority.

'Morning Merula, how are you today?' he said, hoping that his pleasant greeting might divert this bird's attention, as clearly he was anxious about something.

Wasting no time, Merula replied in his hoity voice. 'Percy, have you heard the gossip this morning? The birds in the next garden are saying that Corax has turned the sea black, killing hundreds of our species. Is it true?' He hesitated for a split second, starting to hop up and down the table. 'And, another thing, did you know that Rufus is missing? You must have noticed? What on earth do we do now?' he rattled, as Blackbirds do.

Percy, unsure which question to answer first, and never trusting of Blackbird reporters replied, 'Merula, calm yourself down, I am sure it's not all that bad? Rufus will return,'

'Bad? It sounds like a flapping disaster! Anyway, you know what they are saying? That Corax will eventually take over the whole of Northern Territory, changing our lives forever. Generations of his family have always believed they are the rightful guardians on earth of Mother Nature herself and not Lord Morus. Honestly, if he can create a deadly black sea, maybe he is telling the truth?' Hoping for a reaction, Merula concluded. 'Commander Bewick stands no chance of defending Lord Morus's lands here in the North now. What have you got to say about that?'

'Nothing. Now, that's enough,' Percy said, getting weary of bossy Songbirds and trying to avoid eye contact. 'Anyway, I am sure Rufus will return soon and he'll know what to do here, he always does,' he said, with a slight tone of sarcasm.

'He's young, barely a year old, how is he going to know what to do? He shouldn't really be in charge anyway. Mind you, we need him to turn up soon or you know what will happen?'

Percy nodded and explained, 'Yes, I am well aware of what will happen. Robin Law states that a Robin must always be located within a garden territory. If no Robin is present, the territory is seen as available to all other Robins,' he paused for a moment in deep thought. 'I am surprised we haven't seen any other Robin arrive here and begin to claim it as their own? Having said that, this territory has been in Rufus's family for generations, so it is very strange that he appears to have abandoned us, especially in these dangerous times. But, I feel certain, he will return,'

'Honestly, who ever made the decision to put the Robins in charge? Robin Law…tut! They may understand a bit of a squawking that the 'Beings' speak, but really is that all they can do?' Merula questioned, as he suddenly began to stare at the Being's House at the bottom of the garden, which had distracted him. 'Right now, it would be really useful to know why the Beings haven't fed us yet, like they are supposed to?'

Percy coughed authoritatively, as if pre-programmed, 'Merula, do please call them 'Human Beings' when you spread any news, as that is their proper title and I am sure they will feed us all soon.'

'Unlikely Percy. And by the way, everyone calls them "Beings",' he corrected impatiently.

A second later both birds were aware that they had been joined on the bird table. Landing with a confident thump, a small bright red chested Robin stood proud, her eyes fixed firmly on Merula and Percy, oozing impatience. Her brown wings ruffled by the cold breeze, their tips a little fluffy, indicating she was only in her first year.

Percy braced himself, as he heard Merula whisper. 'I think someone was listening to you Percy! Looks like you got what you wanted.'

'That's enough Merula,' Percy replied, as he watched Merula hop with determination towards the Robin.

'Let's get this over with then. Where are you from? What is your name and most importantly, are you male or female? It's always so hard to tell, as you all wear the same feathers,' Merula demanded to know, clearly considering himself to be used to dealing with Robins, whilst at the same time making Percy wince with embarrassment.

'How rude!' exclaimed the Robin. 'My name is Skyla, I'm clearly female and where I am from is actually none of your business,' poking her tail feathers in the air as she spoke.

Percy hopped forward, pushing his chest out with importance and attempting to mediate the situation. 'Please forgive Merula, my dear. Now, how can we help you?

'I am looking for Rufus, is he here?' Skyla asked in her North East accent, scowling at Merula as she did so.

Rather taken aback, Percy replied quickly. 'Rufus is missing I'm afraid, we haven't seen him for a while.'

"Missing,"…you say? But he asked me to meet him here?' Skyla said, clearly shocked by the news.

Percy paused for a moment to consider his answer; just as he was about to speak, Merula's patience broke.

'How do you know Rufus then? Care to tell us? Did you meet in the bushes maybe?' teased Merula, who always enjoyed winding up Robins, as it was such an easy game to play.

Skyla spun around and looked Merula straight in the eye.

'We are friends, that's all. And, again, it is none of your business,' she snarled back.

'Friends? So, you're not here to fight to claim this territory then?' Merula asked, surprised.

'No. Why would I want Rufus' territory?' Skyla replied abruptly.

Never, in all his years had Percy met a Robin who didn't

instantly wish to start a fight or claim a territory as their own. This female Robin seemed different though. Yet, being a member of the Royal Pigeon Messenger Service rules needed upholding, even if it was Robins who had created the laws in the first place. So, he pulled his silvery wings over his chest, stretched his neck to expose more of his white collar and began to explain. 'Look around you, my dear. You are the first Robin to land here since Rufus left. I am sure you understand how Robin Law works?

'Yes, of course I do,' Skyla said, fidgeting with her wings as she did so and avoiding Percy's gaze.

'So, you are aware of what needs to happen next?' Percy asked, wondering whether she was telling the truth?

'What do you mean?' Skyla asked, appearing nervous.

'A Robin that doesn't understand their own law? Well, I've never met one like you before,' Merula joked, unable to contain his interest in the young Robin.

Percy hopped forward, standing between Skyla and the over excited Blackbird reporter.

'Around here, Robin Law is clear. It states that the first Robin to appear within a territory without another Robin present, must do one of two things. Either another Robin appears and they fight for the territory, or as in your case, you become our Leader until Rufus appears again. It is as simple as that,' Percy officially explained.

'Oh no. That's not why I came. Rufus wouldn't want me to rule his territory. No, no. He simply had a message for me, that's all. Really Pigeon, I am not interested in his territory. Anyway, won't he be back soon? Surely Rufus would never abandon his territory intentionally?'

exclaimed Skyla, clearly beginning to feel the weight of responsibility.

'You are right, Rufus has never left his position before. We need to find him and while we do, this garden needs Robin Leadership,' Percy announced, watching Skyla doing her best to appear in control.

'Well, I really don't think I am the Robin you need. I must be going now. Perhaps you could let Rufus know that I called by?' Skyla said, gingerly hopping backwards.

'Skyla, I am sure it won't be for long and it is your species, who after all, invented this law in the first place?' Percy reminded her, tilting his head to charm her as best he could, watching the realisation dawn on her face that, for now, she needed to stay exactly where she was.

'Shall I show you to Rufus's nest then, 'me' lady?' Merula called out sarcastically, loving the fact that he appeared to have the upper claw over a Robin.

Chapter 5

The Northern Station

Rising a little higher in the sky, offering increasing warmth, the sun had now started to make an appearance over the glistening waters of the Northern Station. Its golden glow of light blanketed the soggy land, whilst its energy began to wake every bird who had spent the night nestling in the grassy reed beds surrounding the lake.

Small flocks of Ducks, Geese and Songbirds started to emerge from the lakeside banks. Some flew straight up into the air stretching their wings, making loud honking noises to welcome in the dawn, whilst others took to the water for their morning search for food, eager to feel the warmth of something delicious dropping into their tummies.

A Squadron of Starlings silently landed around a large clump of tall thick frozen green reeds lying beside the water's edge. Carefully, one Starling Officer stepped forward and parted the reeds, exposing a very smartly coloured Mallard Duck, who appeared to be asleep. His head snuggled deep into the feathers on his back.

Hopping backwards, the Officer delicately coughed in order to wake his Captain with some dignity.

'I was not asleep, Officer. I am merely resting my eyes,' remarked Captain Mallard, his eyes remaining shut as he spoke, his breath appearing like smoke against the morning air.

After a few moments the Captain stretched his shiny green neck, ruffled his brown feathers and rose to his full height. His bright orange legs looked out of proportion to his rather large webbed feet, which squelched in the mud as he began to inspect the Squadron.

One by one the ten Starling Officers stood together in a long line, looking straight ahead, displaying their respect for their Captain.

'Well, what did you find?' the Captain asked gently, having noticed the sad expression as one of his Officers raised their heads.

'Sir, you must prepare yourself, as never have we seen such scenes across our lands,' he said plainly, watching the colour drain from his Captain's face as he gave his account of the disaster scene.

'Corax? He has created a deadly black sea?' asked the Captain in amazement.

'It certainly looked that way Sir, it was like nothing we

have ever witnessed before. Hundreds could be dead, this could mean there are barely any of us left in the North now. He could wipe us out entirely if he wished. Anyway, the whole of that area is useless to our species, probably forever.'

'How quickly was it moving Officer?' questioned the Captain, trying to make sense of what he was hearing, whilst hiding the panic starting to flow through his body.

'Slowly Sir, little by little,' replied the Officer, nervously beginning to fidget with his brown specked wing feathers.

'Slowly?' repeated the Captain, 'well at least that's something I suppose. Has it reached the estuary?'

'No, not yet Sir, but there is no guarantee that it won't though,' explained the Officer carefully, realising the enormity of what he was saying.

Captain Mallard straightened his back and arched his head, 'I knew Corax wished to take over these lands but never did I believe he had such evil ability in him. How could he have created a deadly black liquid?' he sighed, deep in thought.

'We are not sure yet, Sir,' the Officer replied, as he lowered his head with concern.

'If it reaches the estuary, it will have nothing holding it back from flowing down stream to the Northern Station. How can we ever stop Corax? The lands he now governs surely far outweigh that of Lord Morus's ownership. I shall need to inform Commander Bewick immediately.'

'Yes, Sir,' the Officer said, his head still lowered.

The Captain started to plod up and down, 'This is a grave situation indeed…do you have anything else to report?' he asked, hoping they wouldn't.

'No Sir. Only that the Beings were at the scene, chirping at each other as usual. They seemed to be pulling our dead birds out of the blackness, soaked in sticky goo and putting them onto trays. They then took them away,' the Officer informed, as he lifted his head.

'Beings? Taking our species? Where?' interrupted the Captain.

'It was hard to tell, maybe inside one of the large boxes they live in?'

'Why?' snapped the Captain, knowing the Officer Starling couldn't answer that question and he moved on…

'This is ridiculous. As one cloud passes we are being forced out by Corax's Army, as another one goes by we are being chased by a deadly black sea. Let alone being terrified of starving to death because the spring hasn't arrived yet.'

'Sir, we are doing all we can to find any sign of the spring, I assure you,' the Officer did his best to confirm.

Unconvinced, the Captain carried on, 'And Rufus Robin, did you find him?'

'No Sir, not one sign I'm afraid,' the Officer said, watching his Captain re-arranging his feathered wings, clearly getting them ready for flight.

'The Commander will not be happy. I must go to him now, all Squadrons dismissed,' the Captain announced, bringing an end to their conversation.

* * *

The Captain watched as his Squadrons took to the sky and flew over to their official roosting grounds at the other side of the lake. For a moment, he enjoyed the peace as he scanned his home that was so dear to him, but which now felt so very vulnerable.

Immersing himself into the cold lake, he instantly smelt its fishy waters as his webbed feet paddled him along. As he swam by, many of the birds within the hustle and bustle of life on the bankside nodded their heads in respect to him.

Approaching the muddy banks at the opposite side of the lake, he looked up noticing the elegant shapes of two white Swans sitting proudly on a rock that dominated the whole Northern Station.

Climbing out of the freezing waters, the Captain could sense the atmosphere was strained, as light rain started to fall.

As the Captain bowed his head in respect, the larger Swan came straight to the point, his military curt Eastern European tones sounding demanding as he spoke, 'Any sign of the spring yet, Captain?'

Knowing his news would not be welcomed by his Commander, the Captain spoke each word sensitively. 'No Sir, not one I am afraid. Indeed, until the drier weather comes we are unlikely to see new growth or food to eat before then.'

'This is not to be', he gasped, his black eyes peering over his orange beck. 'What on earth am I supposed to do, Captain? Lord Morus, guardian of the natural world, awaits my signal every year that spring has arrived in the north. It allows him to have the confidence of letting the Spring Equinox go ahead, knowing there will be food for us all. But now, what will happen?'

'Commander Bewick Sir, I understand, we must remain

hopeful that the spring will come. Our regiments will continue to search for the signs I can assure you,' the Captain sighed and began to scratch the mud with his orange webbed feet, signalling there was more bad news to come.

'What is it, Captain? Speak up,' shouted the Commander, eager for more information.

Trying to hide his fluster, the Captain did his best to relay the Starling's report in as much accuracy as he dared, watching carefully, as the fear grew in the eyes of his Commander and that of his beautiful partner who stood elegantly beside him.

'Corax? Corax's Army is responsible for this atrocity? That is pure evil,' replied the Commander, aghast.

The Captain sighed, 'Yes, Sir. They were spotted at the scene. There was nothing that could be done. The whole place became too poisonous, our regiments couldn't fly without immediate danger to their own lives.'

'No, no, no! This is too much,' exclaimed the Swan, thinking out loud, 'I am not so sure, Captain, maybe this wasn't the work of Corax, …maybe it is far worse than we could ever imagine?'

'Far worse, Sir?' questioned Captain Mallard, not quite sure where the conversation was heading.

Commander Bewick lowered his head, 'For years now, I have watched as our lands have been degraded and destroyed, our species nearly wiped out. It is only a matter of time now before her ladyship sends us a sign of her anger and disapproval at this destruction.'

'Her ladyship?' asked the Captain, hoping it wasn't an obvious question.

'Yes, Mother Nature herself. Her very spirit is within our lands, seas and our skies,' he paused. 'Maybe the black sea is a sign of her anger?'

'Are you saying Mother Nature herself created the black sea and not Corax?' The Captain questioned, surprised by what he had heard. 'I find that hard to believe Sir.'

'You are right…I hope,' the Commander paused. 'It is more than likely to be the evil work of Corax. We must do all we can to defend this Northern Station, as no doubt we are next.'

'Trust me Sir, this is the work of Corax. I believe what my Regiment has seen. We will do everything within our power to protect this Station, you have my word,' expressed the Captain, hoping it would sound convincing enough for his Commander.

'Good, we must make sure every bird is safe,' the Commander hesitated, looking up to the wintery sky above.

'Sir, I must also tell you that a Robin Leader is missing. We believe it could be Rufus.' The Captain added.

The Commander swung his head quickly and glared at the Captain.

'Rufus? I told him not leave his garden territory! He had one chance to prove himself, just one. I should have known he was too young to care about his responsibilities, and now it is likely his death will be on my head.'

'Sir it is not your fault. We all assumed he could be trusted, given who his father was. Anyway, maybe he is still alive,' the Captain said, hoping it would turn out to be true.

The Captain watched as his words seemed to send the Commander into a momentary trance, staring straight ahead as he spoke.

'I have travelled this world, fought battles and led battalions. Yet nothing could have prepared me for a winter such as this. We must be grateful that the snow no longer falls I suppose?'

'Snow Sir?' the Captain questioned, worrying if he would be expected to already know.

'You have never heard of snow, Captain? Decades ago. rain used to fall as icy flakes or so I am told. Now, our winters are full of this rain, continual rain,' he answered in exasperation.

'Sir, the spring will come,' the Captain said, hoping to reassure his master.

'Yes, yes. Anyway, we need to inform Lord Morus as soon as possible of everything that has happened. It is likely we will need his reinforcements from the south to help us protect what is rightfully his. Do you understand me?' he finished, his curt accent appearing to strengthen as he fought to stay calm.

'Commander, are you sure? Never has the Northern Station asked for help in this way, we have always defended ourselves,' the Captain explained, a little crestfallen.

'Asking for help is not a sign of weakness, Captain. Anyway, as odd as it may sound, I hope Corax is behind this, as the alternative doesn't warrant thinking about,' he answered, thinking aloud.

'Sir?' the Captain questioned, worrying that his Commander still wasn't truly convinced that Corax was the culprit.

'Never mind. For now we must do what we can. Go, make sure our regiments evacuate as many communities as possible in the path of this dangerous black sea and bring them here. And, Captain, make sure the Nightshift do the same. We must work together,' he suggested, and then added. 'Was there anyone else who witnessed this devastation?'

'The Beings were there, Sir. I am afraid to say they were seen pulling our species from the blackness and,' he hesitated, 'taking them inside their large box on the cliff edge.'

'Why?' questioned the Commander.

'It is not clear, Sir,' he paused hoping that the Commander would not question him further on this.

The Commander sighed in exasperation.

'Do all you can, Captain, to save as many lives as possible. And, don't forget to console the mammals on my behalf. They are likely to have lost many of their species as well. Does their Rabbit Leader, Dolores, know?'

'I believe so, Sir,' he replied.

'Good. Now make sure you also warn the Nightshift to be careful what they eat tonight, our smallest creatures maybe full of the black poison themselves. Now, go. You have a lot to achieve,' instructed the Commander.

Above them, the rain clouds darkened and the winds started to pick up, bringing with them a strange fumy smell, which left a smoky taste in their mouths. As the residents of the Northern Station began to cough, they looked to the skies above them, which governed their every day.

* * *

The sun dazzled Rufus Robin's eyes as he flew fast through

the leafy green trees in the woodland at the back of his garden territory. His wings lightly touched the edges of each branch as he dodged in and out of the trees. He knew the flight path so well that he could do it with his eyes closed. Left, right, left, right, oh the joy of flying! Feeling completely free, the air lifting his tiny wings. He could fly faster and then slower, twisting and turning, his red chest being energised by the sunshine. Nothing in life felt as good as this. The ability to fly was a pure blessing from Mother Earth herself.

Occasionally as he looked down, he would see the most inviting dark, moist areas under the small bushes, which helped make up the floor of the woodland. Oh, how he loved dark places where he could hide and find juicy grubs.

Ahead of him he saw Skyla slipping out of the small gap in the leaves, high up in the trees. She joined him and together they darted in and out of the trees, giggling and laughing as they went.

Suddenly his wings felt tired, heavy and began to drag him down. Panic filled his body, as the more he flapped them the heavier they seemed to become, dragging him down, down, down…

Rufus woke up abruptly from his nightmare, feeling disorientated. He tried to open his eyes too quickly, and they stung with pain. The sounds and smells of the Beings' world, in which he found himself, rattled through his immobilised body. Somehow, he had to escape…

Chapter 6

Corax

'Tobias Sir, everyone looks in position below,' a dark Raven croaked to a much larger Raven flying up front. As together they flew under a misty skyline, surveying the gloomy landscape below them.

'Good, if only our rightful Lord 'Corax' could see the stronghold he has across these lands now. Commander Bewick's authority weakens as every cloud passes,' he chuckled evilly, flapping his black shiny feathers to gain more height.

As they flew over towns, villages and a spaghetti-like network of roads, they continually noticed long lines of Corax's Army appearing to control the areas.

As Tobias flew by, each bird nodded in respect, confirming their control of that part of the landscape.

'Every bird is in place. Let's head back,' said Tobias, as they banked to the left and started to head across the freezing skies towards the coast.

Upon reaching the sea, they began to head north up the rugged coastline. Flying directly over the blackened disaster site, concealed by an eerie blanket of sea mist, created by the deadly fumes rising into the sky above.

Flying low, Tobias noticed an even greater gathering of Beings than he had seen when the disaster had first struck. As their anxious calls filled the polluted skies, he chuckled to himself sarcastically, 'They look busy.'

A little farther up the coastline, the tops of an ancient ruined castle could be seen poking out of the mist, its human inhabitants long gone.

Tobias and his friend circled high above the castle walls for a few moments, peering into its ruined towers, waiting for permission to land.

'Tobias, have you any news?' echoed a loud gravelly voice from below.

'Yes, Sire, everyone is finally in place,' replied Tobias, keeping an eye on his master deep within the tower.

'Then get down here you fool where I can see you,' boomed the reply.

Together they quickly flew down the dark tower, entering its damp cold atmosphere. As they started to become accustomed to the light, they noticed that the nooks and crevices of the old walls were filled with the variety of birds that formed Corax's Army. Each bird wore different coloured feathers, from the Jackdaws with their darkened heads and black wings, to the black and white feathers of the Magpies. On the larger ledges stood several lanky, grumpy looking Herons. Their feathers of white and grey looked silky in the gloomy light of the ancient tower.

Together, the whole colony watched as Tobias floated down the tower, eventually landing to bow down in front of his master below.

Tall and slinky, Corax had clearly seen many battles in life. His black feathers looked oily, as he unfolded his weather-beaten wings to signal silence, never taking his green piercing eyes away from staring at Tobias.

'And?' he snapped impatiently.

'Corax Sire, the strength of your hold over these lands increases by the day. Your Army stands guard on every piece of higher ground across this territory, moving communities out wherever we find them,' informed Tobias, as confidently as he could.

'What about the black sea?' demanded Corax, flicking his wings.

Still hanging his head low Tobias replied, 'It virtually appears at your command, Sire, as it speeds towards the Northern Station clearing the lands of life as it goes. Indeed, I can only assume it wishes to help you rid these lands of Lord Morus's communities as well.'

Corax let out an evil chuckle of satisfaction.

'Well, whoever created it, that's very nice of them indeed. Probably created by the Beings; stupid and inferior species that they are,' he expressed, sending sniggers through his audience.

'That is good news, Tobias, you have done well,' he said, pausing for a moment to dream. 'For centuries my family have fought Lord Morus's rule, if only they could see me now.'

Happy with this compliment, Tobias's confidence grew as he added. 'It won't be long now Sire and all these lands will be yours.'

Corax wriggled his wings, surprising his audience as he continued, 'It's not enough though, not this time.'

Tobias looked confused and nervously replied, 'Sire? We have worked tirelessly for your ownership of these lands, what more can we do?'

Corax wasted no time in replying.

'Much more! Lord Morus will soon have no choice but to leave, yet others exist to fill his space. Do you understand me, Tobias?'

Tobias quickly realised what Corax was insinuating, as his eyes began to sparkle with intrigue.

'You're referring to your distant cousin, I believe?' he suggested, revelling in the fact that he had unusually predicted what his master was thinking. Arching his neck proudly, he watched as Corax carried on.

'Pelecanus's lands in the Southern Hemisphere have already been destroyed in intense heat and violent weathers. Imagine how happy he would be to know that Lord Morus is willing to put the past behind him, and is offering the safety of his lands in north.'

Corax stretched out his dark wings and then thoughtfully folded them again.

'Has he?' Tobias enquired quietly, amazed.

Corax snapped back. 'Of course not, stupid. Think of it though, on arrival he will quickly realise that his stay here has to be brief and that his only choice will be to follow in the wake of Lord Morus. Both the titans of our world must head north to temperatures that far better suit their communities. Then Tobias, and only then, will these lands finally be mine.'

Applause filled the old castle walls, as bits of stone started to crumble under the excitement flowing through the murky dark space.

Tobias hopped forward and hung his head in respect, 'Sire, you inspire us and we are dedicated to you. Forgive me for asking, but Lord Morus and Pelecanus have been enemies for centuries haven't they…?'

'Are you questioning my plans, Tobias?' snarled Corax, as his Army of birds held their breath.

'No Sire, not at all,' Tobias said, fearing what would happen and instantly losing confidence, as he felt Corax's eyes bore into him angrily.

'I assume you're concerned Pelecanus will not believe the tale that safety awaits him? I have one word for you, Tobias, 'blood'. You forget, Pelecanus is a distant cousin of mine. Fear not, he will have no choice but to believe Lord Morus has good intentions. Watch and learn, Tobias, watch and learn.' Corax informed, with an evil glint in his eye.

Tobias listened, as cheers went up around the tower, wings flapped in all directions and for a moment, it felt like the whole tower would crumble under the noise. Looking across at Corax, it was clear he was enjoying every minute of attention. As he stretched out his wings even further, instantly silencing his tower once again. Each bird ready to loyally listen to every word he spoke, as he glazed at the sky above him.

'Right now, we must remain strong and to continue to rid these lands of the vermin that call it home,' he explained, as Tobias noticed a change in his mood as he continued. 'Keep an eye out for any unauthorised flying, especially heading south. As we start to squeeze, Commander Bewick will no doubt reach out to Morus and I don't want him finding out my plans too early, it could ruin everything. Am I understood?'

As all the residents of the castle nodded in agreement, Tobias caught the glare of Corax as he sneered, 'Tobias, we have an invitation to send.'

Chapter 7

Evacuation

The rain began to fall continually, as the light started to fade across 42 Barton Gardens. Skyla Robin sat reluctantly in Rufus's nest at the bottom of the garden, feeling like an imposter. Resting on the branches of an old Beech tree, the nest was sheltered from the worst of the rain. Wrapping her wings around herself to keep out the freezing temperatures, she wondered how long it would be before Rufus returned? And what had he been hoping to tell her? Anyway, what did it matter now she found herself thinking, surely, she should just feel angry at the situation he had placed her in? Goodness knows what her parents would think if they knew she was looking after the garden of a Robin traitor who had abandoned his position? The thought made her shiver, yet she couldn't help but remember how exciting it had been to meet Rufus for the first time. Surely, he wasn't the kind of Robin who would do such a thing?

Constantly scanning the garden for danger, Skyla noticed a small line of Blue Tit Songbirds fast asleep and cuddled up together on the lowest branches of the hedgerow, which ran down one side of the Beings' box. She wasn't surprised to see them, it looked like one of the warmest places in the garden, situated on the ground close to a small hole pumping out smelly warm air from the Beings' box.

For a moment, she wondered what they must think of her having appeared to just turn up out of the blue. If only Rufus had been here to introduce her properly, then she might have gained the authority she now felt she needed to earn.

Abruptly, Percy the Pigeon's urgent cooing interrupted Skyla's thoughts as she watched him land with a clumsy thump on the empty bird table in the middle of the garden. Quickly, he righted himself as she flew towards him.

'Percy, what on earth is it now? Have you seen Rufus yet?' she questioned, firmly.

'No, not yet,' Percy answered.

'Well, I really must be going Percy, my own family will be wondering where I am,' Skyla said, preparing her wings for flight.

'That won't be possible I am afraid Skyla. I am here to deliver an urgent message to 42 Barton Gardens,' Percy announced looking extremely concerned, 'you may wish to brace yourself.'

'Brace myself? What for? Percy what's wrong?' Skyla

demanded instantly, her red chest darkening as her impatience grew.

Skyla watched Percy peering under his wing for the message and then at the top of his most professional sounding voice he announced.

'There is to be an evacuation of this location with immediate effect. The rumours are correct, black waters are flooding down the river, heading in this direction. It is not yet clear who has created them but, never the less, this Community is within the danger zone.'

Skyla froze, her heart nearly stopped.

'Who would do such a thing? That doesn't seem possible, are you sure?' Skyla hopped back in shock, trying to take on board what Percy had said.

'Quite sure. This Community must be ready, as the Starling Regiment is approaching,' Percy said gently.

'Ready for what?' questioned Skyla urgently, finding it hard to handle her new responsibility.

'To evacuate my dear, there is no time to lose. The Starlings are on their way,' answered Percy.

'Surely we can wait for Rufus?' Skyla pleaded, panic rippling through her tiny body.

'Skyla, there is no time. You must lead everyone to safety. Do you understand?' Percy counselled.

Slowly but surely Skyla watched as the garden's anxious bird Community crept out of the hedgerow, clearly having overheard Percy's message. At the back of the queue, Merula the Blackbird looked posed ready to take account of the breaking news as it happened.

For a few moments, Skyla felt unable to move, her mind

frozen with panic. Silence filled the air, as the tension rose. It was clear, there was no way out thought Skyla, she needed to rise the challenge, whether she liked it or not. Taking a deep breath, she fluffed up her wings, pushed out her chest and tilted her tail feathers, oozing as much confidence as she could muster.

'Gather around, Percy has informed me that we are in immediate danger from the black waters heading in this direction. As a friend of Rufus's, and in his absence, Robin law dictates that you must all follow my instructions. Do you all understand?' Skyla announced, hoping that nobody was noticing her trembling legs.

Skyla waited for a moment to gauge the response, as she wondered whether they would need more information, or perhaps what she had given them was enough?' As Merula hopped forward, she braced herself.

'And what are your instructions, your ladyship?' asked Merula sarcastically.

'To evacuate you all,' Skyla simply replied, hoping it would be accepted.

'Evacuate us where?' replied Merula, as the rest of the Songbird Community started to panic around him.

'The Starlings will show us, I am sure. At least we will be far away from the danger zone,' Skyla informed as calmly as she could, watching the panic overflowing and becoming all too much for a small group of multi coloured Goldfinches.

'This is it! The end of life as we know it. Did Corax create the black waters? I bet he did. Save yourselves!' they shouted, knocking into one another with their bright red heads.

'That's enough,' demanded Skyla in true Robin style, trying to take control of the situation and aware that Merula looked like he wanted to ask several more questions. 'Everyone stay calm and listen up. It won't be that bad, I am sure.'

'How do you know?' Merula tested, eagerly waiting for her answer.

'Because, there is always a way. That's what my mother always taught me,' Skyla remarked, as she looked down at a small Blue Tit trembling beside her.

'What is it?' Skyla asked.

'We've never been out of this territory before. So, are you saying we must leave our home forever? What will Rufus say when he returns to find his garden empty…he will return though, won't he?'

'Yes,' Skyla replied wearily in all the commotion, 'you're right, of course Rufus will return. But he would not want you all in harm's way, now would he? Right, come on everyone….'

'Your attention please, I require immediate silence,' a voice suddenly sounded causing every bird to turn around to see who could have made such a statement.

Perching proudly, upright and in a long line across the damp roof of the Being's box was the Starling Squadron, their feathers gleaming in what was left of the daylight.

'I am Officer in Charge 126, of the Commander Bewick's Squadron; I demand this territory remains calm,' a very smart looking Starling announced with a serious look on his face. 'Who is in charge here?'

Before Skyla could step forward, one of the other

Starling's shouted, '5.20pm, all change. I'm Officer in Charge 127.'

Clearly well-rehearsed, the Starlings all turned around once and saluted the newly chosen Officer in charge. A routine they performed regularly to keep alert and confuse any predators.

The freshly appointed Officer in Charge scowled down at Skyla looking for an immediate answer. Hopping forward, doing her best to hide the panic which was criss-crossing her tiny body, she announced with as much typical Robin confidence as she could. 'I'm in charge of this garden territory until Rufus returns.'

The Starling Officer in Charge tilted his head, assessing the young female Robin below him, and quickly questioned her as to Rufus's actual whereabouts.

'He's away at the moment. Busy, on an important mission,' answered Skyla, trying to make it sound as convincing as possible.

'Where was the mission taking place?' asked the Officer in Charge.

'You would have to ask Rufus that question. But the last time I saw him, he was flying through that woodland,' pointing with her wing towards the end of the garden.

The Starling Officer in Charge never took his eyes off Skyla, as one of his Squadron whispered in his ear, causing him to freeze and ask. 'Is this the territory of 42 Barton Gardens?'

Skyla nodded, wondering where these questions would be leading her, and continually thinking that she was completely out of her depth.

Straightening his back, the Officer In Charge looked down the row at his fellow Starling Officers, whose slightly drooped bodies all nodded in sadness, predicting the news he was about to deliver.

'It is with regret, that we are to believe your Robin Leader may never return. A poisonous black sea has been discovered, which has taken many lives. It's quite possible Rufus is amongst the dead. We must evacuate your garden territory for your own safety. I have been instructed by your region's Leader, Commander Bewick, to relocate your Community to the Northern Station with immediate effect. You have approximately until...' he stopped and looked at the rainy clouds above him. 'Until that cloud passes over us to collect any belongings you wish to travel with. Nothing heavy or bulky, no twigs, moss or leaves will be accepted in flight,' he finished, watching the resulting shock waves flickering across the tiny faces of the Songbirds in front of him.

'No! He was so young he can't be dead. Not Rufus, surely,' Skyla listened to the garden Songbirds shout, as she felt suddenly sick inside.

'Go, everyone, get ready. You heard the Officer,' Skyla screamed quickly, as she flew up to Rufus's nest to quickly pin down twigs and any leaves that might fly away in the breeze before she could return. Working as quickly as she could, she knew that the faster she moved, the less likely she was to let the surprise feeling of grief overcome her.

As the cloud moved over them, the Starling Officer commanded, 'Into your places everyone, now.'

Skyla flew down to the old bird table in the garden,

which was quickly surrounded by the entire Community, each one watching her every move.

'5.22pm, all change,' as another Officer announced his Leadership. 'I am Officer in Charge 128, everyone ready at my command? We will fly the shortest route to the Northern Station for your own safety. Stay close in flight and be aware, of Beings, squashers and Corax's Army at all times.'

'Get ready everyone, you'll be fine' shouted Skyla, as rain became heavier around them and she finally realised, this time, she was fully in charge.

The current Starling Officer in Charge took in a deep breath, shook the rain from his wings and puffed out his chest.

'In line, we shall have to fly despite the rain,' he shouted and the rest of the Squadron saluted, preparing themselves for flight. 'One, two, three, dive,'

The Squadron of Starlings instantly jumped into the sky in perfect formation, turning in mid-air they headed straight at the Community of Songbirds shouting. 'Follow us, we will protect you, we will protect you.'

Immediately, it was like a gust of wind had swept through the garden as they surrounded every bird and encouraged them up into the air, over the hedgerow and through the gap between the Being's boxes.

CHAPTER 8

THE NIGHTSHIFT

The daylight had nearly disappeared as a lonely wind blew across the lake, skipping across the surface and kicking up the occasional wave as it went by. Any noise of rustling birds in the reeds was drowned out by the swaying of the vegetation on the banks of the Northern Station's main lake. Standing proudly beside the edges of the water stood a large frozen oak tree. Its bare branches struggled to give any protection to two elegant white Barn Owls, perched side by side, on a branch halfway up its trunk.

'Is it time?' one Barn Owl questioned the other, pecking his white and slightly brown speckled wings.

'Alba, you know the drill, we must wait for their sign,' replied the other Barn Owl gently.

'Oh, Canopus, we wait here every night for their signs or messages. The night has almost passed by before the handover happens; they're always running late.'

Both Owls quietly continued to scan the skies for any signs of the official handover that took place every night between the authorities that governed the day, to those which governed the night.

After a while the Barn Owls watched and listened, as other types of Owls began to appear out of the dusky atmosphere, swooping to land on the branches above them.

'Evening all,' said one large brown Owl with long tufted ears and a very deep voice, his weight causing the branch to creak as he landed.

'Good evening,' announced a squeaky voice. At first, the existing three Owls could not identify where the voice had come from. Then, together they noticed a very small, rather grumpy looking 'Little' brown Owl perched on the end of a branch, swaying in the wind.

As they waited for their instructions, it wasn't long before the whispers of gossip began…

'Did you hear?' the Little Owl squeaked to the large brown Long-eared Owl, 'Corax's Army has apparently struck again.'

The Long-eared Owl nodded, 'Oh yes, terrible business, a deadly black sea wasn't it? It is going to be a long night ahead for us, my friend. I am only pleased I managed to find an extremely tasty mouse before I arrived.'

The Little Owl continued, 'I know what you mean. As I flew here tonight, I passed a whole group of Songbirds from a garden, being led by the Starlings through the clouds.

Clearly they were being evacuated. Mind you, at first, I thought it was Rufus's Community, but it was a female Robin who was giving out the orders tonight. Such a bossy species.'

'Well, if you ask me,' the Long-eared Owl said, 'the Dayshift should have sorted this out ages ago. Honestly, what will it take before Commander Bewick acts to stop Corax? It won't take long now for his Army to finally close in on the Northern Station. I mean, we do all we can to protect these lands through the night but it is up to that lot through the day.'

'I agree,' snapped the Little Owl, 'as if our duties are not enough, transporting safely birds here, there and everywhere under the cover of darkness…next we will be looking after the Beings through the night as well,' he finished, sending a chuckle through the other Owls.

* * *

The two Barn Owls below were still searching the skies hoping to see a sign of the hand over, aware that tensions were rising, as the small flock of Owls grew around them.

'Alba, if the messenger doesn't come now our friends below will surely revolt,' Canopus joked as both Owls were relieved to notice what appeared to be a faint blue flickering light coming from the Chamber across the other side of the lake.

Struggling to pull itself free from the wooden walls of the Chamber, the blue light started making its way across the lake towards the Owls. Instantly blown off course by the winds, the light flickered as it battled to stay on its intended flight path.

Finally exhausted, a Dragonfly buzzed into view, its blue body reflecting in the moonlight creating the illusion of a light. Swerving through the wind, it landed precariously on the branch in front of the Owls.

'Phew, that was close,' squeaked the Dragonfly to himself, breathing heavily. Gathering himself, he looked up at the Owls, 'Didn't think I was going to make it….'

The Owls scowled quickly, unnerving the Dragonfly, reminding him that he probably looked quite tasty to them, so came straight to his point…

'Commander Bewick has announced that the night is officially yours, Sir. The Starlings have lined up various species of Songbirds who need to be urgently moved to new feeding grounds under the guidance of the stars, at your command. They are waiting on the south side of the lake for your transporters. I'm afraid to report we have been receiving new communities of birds all through the daylight, terrified of the deadly sea and Corax. Space has become more of a problem,' said the Dragonfly, confidently trying to stick his bony chest out at the same time to add that bit of authority.

Alba sighed and looked to the night sky above, 'Stars? I see no stars just thick black clouds. How are we supposed to know where to fly if we can't see them?'

The Dragonfly began fidgeting, unable to come up with an answer quick enough for Alba.

'Why are you out so early in the year anyway? I wasn't expecting to see you?' Asked Alba.

The Dragonfly quickly replied. 'Didn't you feel that bit of sun this morning, it woke my species.'

'Sun? No, I was sleeping of course,' snapped Alba impatiently. 'Anyway, is that all you have to tell us?'

'No, Sir, I am afraid that's only the start,' replied the Dragonfly nervously, as the Barn Owls began to listen intently as the insect explained everything that he had heard from Captain Mallard only moments earlier.

'...So, you must help us through the night. Corax's Army will surely strike our Station at any time. Most of all though, you must move as many communities as you can away from the danger of the black waters,' the Dragonfly sighed and gathered the last bit of confidence he needed to carry on. 'Also, the Captain wishes you to gather as many Leaders of communities as possible, bringing them to the Chamber as quickly as you can. Commander Bewick himself wishes to speak to those remaining loyal in the Northern Territory as urgently as possible, if we stand any hope of holding onto what is rightfully ours. Oh, and I am to inform you that Rufus, the young Robin Leader is missing. If you come across him, please send him directly to the Chamber.'

The Owls took their time to consider the information they had been given, each folding their wings in thought and staring hard at the Dragonfly.

'Robins are always going missing but never in all my years have I heard of black waters. Are you sure Corax created such a deadly liquid? It just doesn't seem natural?' asked Alba plainly.

The Dragonfly quickly perked up and looked him

straight in the eye, 'What are you suggesting? Why wouldn't it be natural? Even if it is evil?'

'I'm just saying, it is rather odd, don't you think?' he stopped for a moment and seemed to lose his thoughts in the dark sky above.

'Odd Sir?' asked the Dragonfly.

'Forget it,' Alba shrugged, not wishing to enter a deep conversation. 'We will fly tonight, gather as many Leaders as we can to the Chamber, from there we will decide what must be done. Please tell Commander Bewick we will do all we can to help. You are dismissed.'

Feeling immediately relieved of his duties, the Dragonfly took flight back across the dark waters of the lake and disappeared into the distance, his reflective blue light fading as he flew away.

Waiting until the Dragonfly was out of sight, Alba turned to Canopus, ruffling his feathers as he did so.

'Something feels wrong my friend. Surely, Corax isn't capable of such atrocities, not on this scale anyway?'

'I agree. It is an odd coincidence that the spring hasn't arrived yet, that there is hardly any food, and our entire species feels like it's dying out,' replied Canopus, bobbing his head as Barn Owls do, whilst scanning the landscape in front of him, his black eyes flickering in the moonlight.

'This is much darker than we could ever imagine, Commander Bewick must listen before it is too late. Although, I fear we have said these words before and yet nothing ever seems to happen. We always end up trying to pick up the pieces through the night, rescue mission after rescue mission. We even have to find time to bury our dead by moonlight, hunt to feed ourselves and raise our own young as well, as if we have time to do it all?' Alba complained, pushing the rain off his wings with his beak.

'Where would they be without us?' Canopus sighed sarcastically, sinking his head into his chest with importance and raising his beak to the sky.

Alba looked up to the branches, noticing more Owls had arrived to join the Nightshift. Without hesitating he quickly gave out the orders.

'Tawny Owls, take the southern shores of the Station, there's woodland on that side, which I know suits you better and you can transport those that are waiting over there,' he announced. Then turning his whole head entirely to face the Little Owls he asked, 'Take the northern end of the territory, the lands are flatter out there and you can fly faster'.

Alba noticed the rather smug expression on the Little Owl's face as she winked at the Tawny Owls.

'Faster maybe, but not as nimble?' Alba coached. 'Listen, tonight is about working together, not apart. Now, go quickly. Bring together the species Leaders of our territory and any birds that are in danger. Let them know they have no choice, they must attend the Chamber immediately. And, if you could find Rufus, that would be useful as well.'

As the Owls began to flex their wings ready for flight, Alba added one more instruction, 'try not to eat anything poisonous, even the mammals will have been affected by this black sea'.

Silently, they flew off in different directions, leaving the two Barn Owls to their own thoughts, as the sound of the water lapped against the sides of the tree.

'Canopus, do you remember the days when we commanded a whole Parliament of Owls, across the entire Northern stretch of these lands? Now, our area of service has extended, yet we are the remaining few.'

'Next, you'll be remembering the days when the bees were alive,' Canopus replied, as they both flew silently between the raindrops in the night sky.

CHAPTER 9

CAPTURED

'Why, are you even trying to escape?' a voice with a Northern accent questioned.

Bang, bang, bang.

Rufus Robin now felt fully awake and was eagerly bashing the sides of his crate to escape, deep within the walls of the Coastguard's Bird Rescue Centre. His eyes still stung in pain even though he could open them, but his wings felt like stone.

'Hey, are you listening to me?' the voice repeated.

Rufus quickly turned his head, searching for the owner of the voice and immediately made out what appeared to be two large yellow eyes staring back at him, through the bars of his crate. Noticing his bright yellow beak, Rufus's heart sank as he realised he had been captured next to a large white and grey Seagull, who in Rufus's opinion lacked any intelligence and were only interested in one thing…food.

'We are all doomed. You're doomed. I'm doomed. The whole world is doomed. In fact, you may as well give up now,' the Seagull theatrically suggested, much to the annoyance of Rufus, who had already run out of patience.

'Oh, stop your wailing. We're not doomed, just a bit stuck that's all. I'll have us all out of here in no time, just you watch me,' Rufus replied optimistically, hiding the pain he felt from the sore patches under his feathers, where the oil had seeped through to his skin.

Slumped against the side of his box the Seagull said, 'Whatever you say. I mean, Robins are always right. Good luck with all that banging by the way.'

'Thank you,' Rufus replied sarcastically.

'I am Larus, in case you're interested? Robins usually aren't, especially young ones,' Larus said, irritating Rufus.

'What do you mean 'young ones'? I'll have you know I run my own garden territory,' Rufus pointed out as he carried on bashing his crate to escape, which also helped to drown out Larus's sniggering.

'Well, I only hope Commander Bewick doesn't see you in this state, he's unlikely to let you, "run your own garden" again, isn't he?'

Rufus glared as best he could at the annoying Seagull, hoping that his words wouldn't turn out to be true, as it had taken him months to convince the Commander he was old enough to run the garden himself. The last thing he needed was to be placing any doubt in the Commander's eyes of his authority.

After a while, the stinging in Rufus's eyes started to subside, as he began to peer outside the bars of the crate…

'What is this place?'

Larus chuckled, 'You don't know? You do surprise me.'

'Of course, I know…' Rufus lied, feeling the realisation sinking in of where he actually was, which sent pulses of panic racing through his tiny body, '…we're inside a Being's box?'

'Sharp, aren't you? Yes, we are. Still feeling optimistic?' Larus said leaning back on his large white wings, appearing to enjoy watching the panicking Robin in front of him.

'What is that stench?' Rufus said as a strong acid scent wafted through the air, taking him by surprise as he stumbled again over what felt like a feathery ball on the bottom of his crate.

'What the…?'

Looking down at the hard metal floor of his rescue crate, just next to a bowl of water, a grey beak poked through a motionless ball of brown feathers. Rufus bent down beside the bird, peeling back its feathers and trying to establish whether it was alive.

'Brown, cream, feathers,' he said out loud, 'Sparrow, are you alive?'

As there was no immediate response, causing Rufus to quickly conclude.

'You're, you're…dead? No, no, you can't be!'

Falling backwards, Rufus immediately felt sick. Slowly, he backed away from the bird, unable to take his eyes of its lifeless body.

'Arrrh…,' screamed Rufus, releasing the pressure of sadness he felt flowing through his tiny body.

'Shhhhhhhhhhhh!' snapped Larus, 'you'll bring the Beings out.'

'Oh, stop your moaning. He is dead! Dead. Is there anything we can do?' Rufus shouted, hoping someone would come up with a magic answer.

'I doubt it now. Looks pretty dead to me. Anyway, he is just one of the many that we lost last night. We are apparently the lucky ones. Although, am not sure I feel that lucky stuck in here,' Larus said, fidgeting with his wings and watching Rufus for a reaction. 'But, if you keep shouting like that, you will bring the Beings out again and I am not sure you want that, right?'

Rufus ignored most of what Larus had said and returning thoughtfully to the Sparrow's body, he folded its wings respectfully with his beak. Standing for a second, in the hope that perhaps, Mother Nature herself would be taking care of its tiny spirit. Immediately, the painful memory of his own parents deaths came to mind. Quickly, shaking his feathers in the hope it would go away. He turned his attention to the task in front of him, hopping towards the front of the crate.

'I am not frightened of the Beings, why should I be? I just want out of here.' Rufus announced abruptly.

Taking in a large gulp of air, opening his beak as wide as he could and lifting his tail feathers as high as they would go, he began to deliver his signature song.

'What the heck are you singing for?' questioned Larus abruptly.

'It is my song, it's what 'we' Robins are taught to do in times of danger.'

Finishing his song, he turned to look at the Seagull, who was now lying on his side with an inquisitive look on his face.

'I think you might want to work on your song, it is a bit scratchy.'

Sensing another clever comment was coming, Rufus changed the subject.

'I will not give up. I've a garden territory which needs me, I've no time to lose.'

'Look, if you start doing the strutting thing Robins do when you get far above yourselves, then they'll only poke you again.'

'Poke me again'? Rufus asked, remembering how it felt to be held by a Being and the sharp pain which had entered him.

Watching his every move, Larus replied, 'It's no good, you know. You move, they move. Stay still and they won't see you. Anyway, it isn't them who we need to be afraid of is it?'

'What?' snapped Rufus, 'what do you mean?'

'I've been trying to remind you but has last night rang any bells yet? Larus said sarcastically.

Agonisingly, the memory began flooding through Rufus's mind.

'The black sea! The Beings screams, the smoke and darkness. I tried to save as many as I could, but most had died before I could reach them. I tried so hard, but the blackness, I couldn't breathe, I couldn't...I couldn't do anything for them.'

He crumbled to the floor and after a few seconds of

composing himself, he carried on, 'All I had wanted to do, was to find a new place to live for Skyla and my Community… now my parents are gone….,' he stopped himself for a moment. 'Oh no, Skyla! I invited her to call by, what if she came and I wasn't there? You see, there is no food in our garden. Nothing, I just wanted to prove to her that I could find a safer place to live,' he said, shaking his feathers.

'Oh, a feisty female Robin eh? Oh, for the love of a lady Rufus,' Larus sniggered inappropriately.

'Shut up! It is not like that,' Rufus blushed and then carried on, unable to stop the words flowing out of his black beak. 'Anyway, all I found was dead birds everywhere. The sky stank of smoke and I could hardly see anything. In fact…wait. In the darkness, there were birds which looked like…Rooks. Yes, Rooks! The slivering evil Army of Corax. They were there. I remember now. They caused all this pain?' Rufus concluded.

'Steady young 'un,' said Larus, realisation dawning in his eyes, 'that's quite an accusation to make'.

Ignoring him, Rufus began bashing the bars angrily and wondering how he would ever escape.

'Arrh, I need to get out of here and find out what happened. I don't care if they see me,' coughing in the chemical filled air as he did so.

'Will you calm down, you'll wake them and we might end up like him' Larus said, pointing at the motionless Sparrow next to Rufus.

The Beings didn't kill him, the black sea did. Anyway, they won't hurt me, I am a Robin. Our relationship goes back centuries but I can see why you might be worried though,' teased Rufus, remembering being told a rumour that the Beings appeared to dislike his species.

As words flowed out of Rufus's beak, they seemed to give him renewed strength. 'Right, how can I get out of this place?' he said, tapping his beak on parts of the bars which looked like potential weak spots.

'For goodness sake you're going to wake them, you crazy Robin' whispered the Larus again.

Rufus carried on though, 'You're not scared are you, Larus, a big Seagull like you?'

Folding his wings in around himself Larus looked rather worried.

'I don't want a pointy thing up my bottom or anywhere near me, thank you very much. Anyway, they might feed us again soon'.

'Is that really all you think about, food?' Rufus said in a disgusted tone and started to march up and down his box, clearly not worried by the amount of noise he was making.

Suddenly, Rufus felt a small vibration on the bottom of his crate. His heart nearly stopped. He held his breath as he watched the fluffy brown ball of feathers begin to move…

'He's alive!' shouted Rufus, hopping over to the tiny struggling House Sparrow. 'I can't believe it!'

Slowly but surely the brown feathers began to unfold into the shape of a small bird, first the left wing, then the right wing unfolded painfully. Struggling, the grey tips of the Sparrow's head emerged above his feathers, his beak only just poking through. After a few seconds he managed to straighten his body and began stretching his legs, preparing to stand up. Wobbling, he managed to mumble, 'Who is making that horrible noise?'

'What noise?' snapped Rufus, rather unsympathetically, instantly concerned that he could be sharing this crate with an unusually bossy Sparrow, and judging by the size of his dark brown feathers under his beak, clearly a slightly older bird than he was.

'Where on earth am I? This place is even noisier than my family,' the Sparrow shouted, as he started to look around him.

'Err…you've been trapped by the Beings but don't worry yourself, my name is Rufus and I will get you out of here safely,' Rufus stated confidently, appearing to predict exactly what the House Sparrow would wish to hear.

'I am what? Trapped?' The Sparrow panicked as he noticed the Being through the crate's bars at the other side of the room. 'Just be quiet, I'll think of something but whatever you do, don't attract the Beings. Oh, I'm Jack, by the way.'

'Well, Jack. I think you'll find that I will decide and get us out of here, relax,' sniffed Rufus, slightly irritated that this tiny House Sparrow had instantly thought his plan would be better than Rufus's own.

Across the crate, Rufus watched carefully as Jack finally rose onto his claws. For a split second, Rufus noticed what looked like a flash of recognition flicker through Jack's eyes, which instantly irritated him. If there was one thing he was growing tired of, it was the appearance of his small red chest and fluffy wings. Every bird just instantly seemed to assume Rufus was too young to be in control, the sooner he could grow his chest the better.

'Is something wrong?' Rufus assumed.

'No but relaxing is something I am unlikely to do with a Robin hopping around,' replied Jack in an honest manner.

The moment was unexpectedly broken by the noise of the room's door being flung open. A giant Being walked in, wearing a full white clinical looking gown and heading straight for a crate on the worktop in front of him. The birds watched as he covered his hands with gloves, opened the tiny door of the crate and reached inside. His hands seemed to struggle for a while to find its occupants, only to discover that the tiny Blackbird he lifted slowly out appeared limp and asleep.

Rufus, Jack and Larus quietly gasped as the Being started to rub the sleeping bird's chest.

'What are they doing?' questioned Rufus, feeling responsible for the Songbird, as the Being lifted the bird up towards his ear to listen to his breathing.

Larus quickly determined.

'Oh, gee. He's going to eat him alive!'

All three birds watched in amazement as the Being then gently replaced the Blackbird in its crate, closing the door behind it.

'Do you think it might be dead?' whispered Jack.

'Probably is now,' joked Larus, as the main door to the room opened up and a tall female Being walked in causing Rufus to quickly cock his head, as Robins do to enable them to translate the 'Being's' strange language.

As the female began to talk, Larus whispered to Rufus, 'What is she saying?' As, all birds knew that Robins were indeed the only species on the planet that had the ability to understand.

'I'm still learning…shhh,' snapped Rufus, although a few seconds later the content of their conversation started to dawn on him.

'Oh! Surely not?' he trembled, stepping backwards and almost falling over when the Beings had finally finished communicating and left the room.

'What?' shouted Jack, 'what's wrong?'

'Arr…, I think they were talking about hundreds of birds having died. Then, they are saying something about an east-u-ary, what's that?' Rufus loosely translated, 'and a bluuck sea? What are they talking about?'

Jack, who had been listening intently, quickly realised, 'Estuary maybe?' he suggested and then thought for a second. 'There is an estuary near here, right?'

'Yes,' confirmed Rufus, remembering that he had flown over it on the way to the coast, 'what's bluuck though?' he asked, realising Jack might have his uses.

'The black sea maybe? That black sticky glue, which I presume trapped you as well last night?' he suggested and then sighed heavily. 'Honestly, remind me again why Mother Nature blessed Robins with the ability to understand the Beings and not us House Sparrows?'

Rufus fluffed up his feathers and hopped forward, 'Because, Jack, 'We' Robins are the bravest of birds and the stronger species. And the strongest, always wins.'

'All right, you two. Feathers down. I think we might have bigger issues to worry about right now?' Larus interrupted, 'like the black sea maybe?'

'Yes, I hate to admit it but you're probably right,' Rufus said, taking a deep breath, 'If the black sea is moving up the

Estuary…then wait a minute. My garden could be next? Oh, and what if Skyla is there? I have to get out of here now!'

'Yes, well, we will find a way,' Jack said, appearing to look for an escape route, whilst Rufus panicked.

'And…what if the Commander discovers I have left my post and the black sea wipes out my entire Community! He will never trust me again.'

'Rufus, calm down. We will get out of here, we just need to think,' Jack paused. 'Anyway, just think what the Commander will say, when you survive this. I am sure he will forgive you.'

Rufus hadn't thought of it like that, maybe Jack was right?

'Yes, and just wait til I tell him who caused this disaster in the first place,' Rufus imagined,

'Rufus, you don't know Corax did actually cause it,' predicted Larus.

'Wait…Corax caused this?' Jack said, getting involved, 'are you really sure about that?'

'Yes, of course I am sure, did you not see his Army last night?' Rufus replied confidently.

Jack, unsure what to believe, decided to change the subject.

'Well, I was always told that the river might lead to the Station but I can't be sure, I've never flown it. Are you completely sure they said that?'

'Well, I think so. I'm still learning their language. Anyway, what I do know is that we have to get out here, and fast,' he screamed and then quickly started singing again at the top of his voice.

Chapter 10

THE MANX

Surrounded by his Army, Tobias proudly at his side, Corax stood like a statue looking down the estuary's waters in the moonlight as the occasional hail shower fell.

'It won't be long now, Sire, they are due any moment,' Tobias said, sensing his master would become agitated if he waited any longer.

'I have waited all my life for this moment. If a few more clouds pass it will not bother me, I assure you.' Corax replied confidently.

In the unsettled night sky above, they began to see the shapes of a small flock of birds emerging out of the gloom, heading directly for them. As they came closer, their black wings rapidly flapped momentarily and then powering them to glide seamlessly across the tops of the water. Effortlessly, they landed in a triangle formation in front of Corax, the front bird slowly lifting his small head to reveal his feathered white chest.

'My whole life, I have wished to meet a Manx Shearwater and now you are before me. I welcome you all,' slithered Corax.

The Manx, only half the size of Corax, wore an inquisitive expression.

'And you are?'

'My name is Corax and this is my...' Corax started to explain.

'We had been expecting to meet my own cousins the Puffins,' the Manx realised, quickly interrupting him. 'As representatives of Lord Morus's Parliament, they sent us an invitation? Surely, there has been some mistake?'

'Oh, no. No mistake, I assure you. The Puffins are extremely busy, what with the spring equinox approaching and the storms remaining. They asked me to meet you instead. and I am more than happy to step in to assist with their duties. Please be assured you have all the blessings you need.'

Irritated the Manx replied, 'Well, as disappointing as this is, our time is precious, and we must make haste. We have flown directly from Pelecanus himself and his situation worsens as every cloud passes by. You see, his lands across the Southern Hemisphere have burnt out, depleted of food and shelter. His vast communities are on the brink of starvation and urgently seek new lands. Lord Morus's offer of safe lands could not have arrived at a better time, if it is to be trusted of course.'

'Trusted? My dear Manx, it is the truth. Look around you, these are safe lands,' replied Corax, in the hope that the Manx hadn't noticed the fumes that were occasionally drifting through the night air.

With a sceptical eye, the Manx replied, 'I'm sure you understand, Corax, that given the history between them, Pelecanus must receive assurance directly from Lord Morus if he is to begin his flight north. Indeed, if he decides to make this journey it would be the most dangerous flight his communities have ever made and many are likely to lose their lives.'

Tobias turned to look uneasily at his master, wondering what he would say next, yet Corax wasted no time in replying.

'Of course, I understand your concerns. Our world has changed, Lord Morus would want nothing more than to reach out to his spiritual brother in the south, welcoming him in these volatile times and ultimately uniting our fragile planet.' As he spoke, he folded and unfolded his wings, as if trying to look as smart as possible.

The Manx immediately turned to his flock, as they all gathered closely around him whispering nervously for a few seconds before turning back to face Corax.

'Again, what assurances can you offer us that your words speak the truth? The decision we make now will affect the lives of the only remaining bird Community in the south. Their lives are in our claws.'

'Let me reassure you that Lord Morus wouldn't have sent me here, if he didn't trust me. Indeed, you may remind Pelecanus that we are related through our blood and I wouldn't dream of misleading such a valuable member of my family, would I? Believe me, take Lord Morus's blessing with you,' croaked Corax, arching his light brown neck and watching the Manx from the corner of his eye.

The Manx quickly caught a glimpse of the moon as it disappeared behind a dark cloud. 'We must leave now, time is running out to make it safely back. We will inform Pelecanus of your reassurance and in his time of great peril, I am sure he will appreciate Lord Morus's kindness. Although, his arrival here in the North will take some time, as I'm sure you can imagine.'

As quickly as the Manx had finished, the whole flock disappeared back into the night sky.

Tobias couldn't wait a second longer, 'Sire, "Lord Morus's kindness? Are you sure about that?" he asked tentatively.

Corax chuckled to himself, 'Morus will thank me in time, you'll see.'

CHAPTER 11

THE ESCAPE

'It's no good, Rufus. There is no way of escaping, you will have to think of something else,' Larus pointed out, having watched Rufus for some time, consistently banging each bar with his beak to see if there was any obvious weakness in its structure.

'Oh, and what do you suggest?' Rufus snapped back in his eagerness to break free.

'Don't mind me, I am just trying to offer some help. I know you Robins are always sooo right,' teased Larus, as he continued to watch Rufus from the comfort of his own crate, lounging back on his large wings.

'How old are you anyway?' Larus pondered.

Rufus stood up as tall as he could make himself, pushing his red chest out with annoyance.

'I'm old enough, that's all you need to know,' snapped Rufus.

'Alright. I was only asking. You look at bit young to be out here alone, that's all,' replied Larus, starting to enjoy winding up the feisty Robin again.

'My parents died; I had no choice but to take over. I'm old enough now though and quite capable of looking after myself, thank you very much.' Rufus snarled, hoping his words would silence the Seagull.

Rufus carried on banging each bar, as the noise was weirdly helping him ignore the painful memories of his parents which kept leaping into his mind, every time he spoke about them.

'I'm sorry to hear about your parents,' replied Larus, 'truly, I am.'

'Yep, well, it happens right?' confirmed Rufus flippantly.

'I'm sorry too,' added Jack slowly beside him, narrowing his eyes at Rufus, as if deep in thought.

'What?' asked Rufus after a while of starting to feel paranoid about the way Jack was looking at him.

'Nothing, its nothing,' replied Jack quickly looking away.

'Anyway,' Larus continued, 'aren't you Robins supposed to understand those Beings? Why can't you ask them to let us go free instead of all that banging?'

'They don't understand me, it is a one-way thing,' mumbled Rufus, 'anyway, they think we squeak and chirp, honestly why would we do that?'

After a few moments, Rufus finally fell back against the side of his crate in disappointment, letting his eyes wander around his confinement.

'If only I could see how to…,' he began, as his eyes then rested on a piece of the crate which looked out of place. A strange shape appeared to jut out near the front of the crate. Hopping onto his claws, he made his way over and started to poke it. To his surprise it moved easily, so he nudged it again. Quickly, he realised that this odd shape of a latch had been holding closed the front of the cage.

'What the?' Rufus exclaimed in excitement as the front of the cage slowly started to swing open and freedom was in sight.

Seconds later, his excitement quickly turned to pure fear as the door of the room went bang and in wandered a Being, causing all the birds to instantly freeze in their crates. Helplessly, he hoped it wouldn't attract the Being's attention, as the crate door continued to creak and groan as it freely opened itself.

Mumbling to himself, the Being didn't appear to have noticed and walked past the crates towards the other side of the room, wafting his chemical smell up Rufus's nostrils and making him cringe.

The birds watched eagerly as the Being spent a few moments tidying some equipment, picking up a book and heading for the comfort of an old blue chair in the corner of the room. Letting out a huge yawn, he then began quietly looking at his book whilst rubbing his eyes.

Rufus seized the moment, urgently trying to get Jack's reluctant attention.

'Psst…Jack. We should get out of here, come on we could save everyone.' Much to his irritation, it appeared as though Jack was ignoring him.

'Hey Jack. Come on, we could save everyone. I have an

idea but I need your help,' Rufus tried again, yet still Jack seemed to be looking deliberately the other way.

'I've nothing to say to you,' finally Jack replied bluntly, surprising Rufus.

Trying to ignore the comment Jack had made, Rufus carried on.

'Fine, but I'm going to need your help if we are to save everyone?'

'I didn't know Robins accepted help from such lowly creatures as House Sparrows,' Jack snapped.

It never took much for a Robin to lose his temper and Rufus was no different.

'What is wrong with you suddenly?'

'What's wrong? What's wrong! Don't you remember me?' shouted Jack, as Rufus turned to bash his frustration out on the lock.

'Err, what Jack? What are you talking about? We don't have time for this,' snarled Rufus, quickly realising Jack wasn't going to move fast enough as his patience ran out. Maybe Larus, who had been keeping a watchful eye on the situation, would help instead he thought?

Whispering slowly to the large Seagull, Rufus explained, 'I can save everyone here, but I need your help. Keep an eye on that Being and if he moves then cause a distraction, do you understand?'

'Are you having a laugh, what type of distraction did you have in mind?' grunted Larus.

'Do I look like I'm joking?' demanded Rufus. 'Jump about or something, flap your wings. I don't know but do whatever you can to help us get out of here, and fast.'

'Oh, no, no, no,' urged Larus, 'that's a crazy idea, Robin.'

'Look, we have no time. If that black sea reaches the river, goodness knows what damage it will do. Are you listening to me? Get up,'

Larus's eyes flickered with what appeared to look like compassion.

'Come on,' Rufus shook his head in despair and wrapped his wings around the bars in front of him. 'Come on, I have to get home. I need to see if Skyla is ok and that my Community is safe.'

Once again, he turned to look at Jack, hoping that his speech would have ignited his interest, as House Sparrows were known for their caring characters, yet clearly not this one Rufus quickly concluded.

'All right, all right, I'll save the day then,' announced Larus sarcastically. Reluctantly, he threw himself on his back and began wailing.

'No, not yet! I'm not ready,' screamed Rufus, not expecting the Seagull to be so dramatic, so quickly.

Instantly the startled Being jumped up from his chair and ran across the room towards the distressed Seagull. Seconds later the door of the room flung open and other Beings came running in to help.

Rufus found himself with no choice, it was now or never as he started to fly around the room, bashing the latches on the crates and allowing the doors to swing open.

'See what you've done,' he heard Larus call just moments before the Beings poked him with a long sharp needle, rendering him limp on the floor within seconds.

'Oh, you've done it now!' shouted Jack, suddenly getting

involved and flying out of the crate after Rufus who was continuing to successfully release as many birds as he could. The deafening sounds of their squawks filling the room, causing several more Beings to come crashing through the door, their faces dropping at the sheer scene unfolding in front of them.

Rufus and Jack watched in horror as several very disorientated birds started hitting the walls and landing in heaps on the floor.

'Rufus, they'll be squashed. Head for that gap in the wall, show them the opening!' shouted Jack.

Rufus wasted no time and flew straight towards a window, which was slightly ajar at the top. Jack followed and together they managed to force the window down a bit further. Seconds later, a stream of birds started to fly through, screeching with delight as they felt the freedom of the fresh air. From Doves to tiny Blue Tits, each bird stretched out their mangled oily looking wings, forcing them to work as they attempted to fly up their only escape route.

'Come on, Larus, wake up, fly,' shouted Rufus, as the big ungainly Seagull started to come alive again from his dopey state and attempt to unfold his large white wings. Misjudging the end of the table he had been put on, he fell to the floor with a bump.

'Larus,' shouted Rufus, 'get up, come on, you can do this.'

Somehow the huge Seagull managed to stand up, instantly spreading his strong white wings as he headed towards the window at speed. By luck, rather than judgement, he managed to dodge the grasping hands of the

Beings and launch himself through the opening with both Rufus and Jack in hot pursuit.

Cold fresh wind hit the birds instantly, as they forced themselves into the gigantic morning sky. Below them, the air was full of screaming birds, flapping wings and feathers flying in all directions.

'To freedom!' shouted Rufus, 'Fly.'

Looking down behind him, Rufus stopped immediately, flapping to keep airborne. Panic raising through his body, something was wrong. The escaping birds had begun missing their escape gap, smashing into the walls and tumbling into the puddles at the foot of the building. Their blackened wings weighed down by the sticky black goo which was still holding them together, panic flickered through their eyes, as they began to lose the battle to survive.

'Come on, save yourselves,' Jack encouraged, as their squeals rang out though the sky.

Realising he must do something, Rufus shouted, 'Wait I'm coming,' and began folding his feathers, ready to plummet to their rescue.

Out of nowhere, pain struck his wings, as he was dragged high up into the sky against his will.

'Come on, you can't save them now, it is too late,' Larus shouted, as it took all of his strength to control Rufus's wriggling.

'Get off me! Let me go. I failed them last time and I won't let that happen again.' screamed Rufus.

'Look at them, they're covered in the black stuff. There's no hope for them now, leave them to the Beings,' cried Jack, attempting to help Larus.

'No, no, I have a duty to help them,' Rufus shouted

angrily, still trying to pull himself free and watching below as the Beings began picking up the dying birds below.

It was a while before Rufus stopped struggling and shouting at Jack and Larus. Eventually, trusting that he wouldn't dive for the earth, they released their grips and all three birds floated for a moment.

'We're too high,' identified Jack, suddenly feeling light headed. 'If we hit the Skyway like this we are going to be in serious violation of our agreed flying height. We need to head back down' he said, realising he had never flown so high before.

Exhausted, the three birds allowed their bodies to slowly float down towards the grey earth below, as they eagerly looked for somewhere safe to land.

CHAPTER 12

TARGET

A little while later, deep within a dark woodland, Rufus, Jack and Larus were an unlikely sight balancing together on the branches of an old Sycamore tree, as it gently swung from side to side.

The silence between them spoke louder than any words, which was matched by the expressions of sadness on their faces.

It was Rufus who made the first move, shaking his brown tiny wings and stretching his bony legs, as Jack watched him with a keen interest.

'Come on, we're wasting time,' Rufus announced turning to look back at Larus and Jack. 'We saved every life we could, now we must reach the Commander urgently to let him know what has happened. I don't want him thinking that I have abandoned my garden.'

'You've changed your tune,' criticised Jack, rubbing his wings and wincing as he did so.

Rufus wasn't listening, as he was busy smelling the air and attempting to get his bearings of where they had landed. Eager to get a better view of the woodland, he hopped down the branch so that he was positioned on the tips of its spindly ends. It was a trick he had learnt from watching other Robins in near-by communities, assuming that's what his Dad is likely to have approved of as well. "Always be on guard and the first to spot danger," is probably what Dad would have said, thought Rufus, as that painful feeling of losing his parents swept through his tiny body once again. It seemed so unfair that he had never really got the chance to know them properly, or to learn Robin Law through them, the way he should have done.

Unexpectedly, all three birds felt something quickly change in the atmosphere of the woodland itself. The wind seemed to stop abruptly, the leafless trees appeared to stand silent and time slowed down.

A shiver raced down Rufus's spine and panic started to fill his feathers, as his black eyes darted in every direction, eagerly trying to find out what had caused it. Rufus looked across, noticing Jack's captivated face and wondering what he had seen. Seconds later, he also spotted the predator, turning his Robin blood cold.

Together, the birds watched in horror as a Grey Sparrowhawk, with an evil determination in its eyes, flew through the trees towards them, looking for its next kill.

'Stay still, whatever you do don't move,' Jack whispered feebly, 'maybe he won't see us if we hide behind these branches?'

It was too late though, and within seconds the piercing yellow eyes of the Hawk had locked firmly down on its prey.

'Rufus, watch out!' Jack shouted, 'he is looking directly at you.'

Momentarily, shockwaves immobilised Rufus's body. There was only one thing he felt he could do. Widening his beak and producing the highest pitch he could, a squawking flute like tune left his lungs.

'What the heck are you doing?' whispered Jack.

'In times of danger, my weapon is my song,' shouted Rufus with confidence, then quickly changing his mind when he saw Jack's shock ridden face, 'but maybe not this time…'

Travelling at a tremendous speed, weaving effortlessly in and out of the trees, the Sparrowhawk started to angle its bluey grey wings, and white and black stripy chest at just the right shape to attack.

Faster than lightning, Jack surprised Rufus by launching himself directly at him, his impact knocking them both of their perches. As the Sparrowhawk just missed them, the sheer power of the bird left a slip stream, flipping Jack and Rufus up into the air, tumbling towards the ground. For a spilt second, Rufus thought he heard it whisper, "go, you don't belong here."

Screaming, both birds used all their strength to try and right themselves in the air, tensing their bodies ready for the pain of impacting the hard soil below. Yet to their surprise, they landed on the soft white wings of a large Seagull.

'Larus!' they shouted, clinging to his wings. He clumsily flew as fast as he could towards the edge of the woodland, hoping the Hawk wouldn't decide to have another attempt at having its lunch.

Seconds later, all three birds landed with a thump behind a large bush by a stone wall on the edge of the trees, exhausted.

Rufus instantly started shaking his wings and looking for the next flight path, feeling ashamed that Jack and Larus had saved his life. Usually, it was Robins that did the lifesaving, not House Sparrows and especially not Seagulls.

'They should be called Robin Hawks, not Sparrowhawks,' Jack jested, 'and by the way, I think the word you're looking for is 'thank you,' Rufus?' he pointed out, patting Larus gratefully as he did so.

'What? Oh, yes, err thank you,' Rufus blurted out in a rather uncomfortable fashion. 'Did you hear it whisper something?'

'Tricky to say, as we looked death in the eye. Did you?' Jack joked.

'I'm not sure. Oh well, come on, this is wasting time, we need to get out of here,' fluffing his feathers to assert his importance.

'I want to stop by my home territory and check everyone is safe, it is on our route anyway.'

Jack, still out of breath replied with sarcasm, 'Home?'

Rufus's patience suddenly broke, 'Yes, "home". What's your problem with that, Jack?'

'My problem? Unlike you, we don't have a home, do we? I was trying to move my family to live by the sea, yet I lost contact with them. Goodness knows where they are now, and here I am saving you. And his home…,' Jack said, pointing at Larus, 'was probably on the cliffs, which now stink and are covered in black goo.'

Determined, Jack continued, 'And, whilst I think of it, you still don't recognise me properly, do you?'

Rufus spun around to look Jack in the face, trying to understand why he was being so irritating, especially when their lives were still in danger.

'What?' he snapped, as a memory began to niggle him at the back of his mind.

'It was painfully cold, surely you remember defending your territory from a starving House Sparrow and his partner?' Jack quickly took the opportunity to remind him. 'Such a brave thing for you to do, did your Community applaud you? Did they?' Jack trembled with anger as his words flowed out.

Sure enough, a vivid memory stopped Rufus in his tracks, as he realised where he had seen Jack before. The winter had been harsh and he remembered how he had felt one day about guarding the only food which had been left out by the Beings, saving it for his own Community.

Taking in a deep breath he began, 'Jack, I am so sorry. I remember you now,' Rufus paused, 'I didn't have a choice, there wasn't enough food to go around.'

'We almost starved, how can I forgive you for that?' snapped Jack.

'I was barely a few months old, what was I supposed to do?' Rufus protested, fighting the feeling of responsibility that always seemed to land on him.

'Feed us? Isn't that what you Robins are supposed to do?'

'I couldn't, Jack, the Beings hardly ever put anything out for us and there's nothing in the land around.'

'What about your song? Isn't that how every Robin is trained, to sing for the Beings attention? You know, to remind them of their responsibility.'

Rufus looked away in embarrassment, 'I couldn't, I didn't know how.'

'Why?' demanded Jack in a deliberately unfeeling way.

'Because my parents never had the time to show me before they died. I barely knew them. I had to learn everything myself. Happy now, are you?' Rufus shouted emotionally, dropping his head and awkwardly kicking the soil about.

It took a few awkward seconds for Jack to eventually break the silence.

'I am sorry you lost them, Rufus; I didn't mean to….'

'Oh, forget it, Jack, like you care,' interrupted Rufus, wishing to change the subject, 'anyway, you're still alive, aren't you?'

Jack immediately looked offended and refolded his wings.

'Yeah, no thanks to you! I need to get out of here and find out what's left of my family,' he announced after a few moments, starting again to fluff his wings ready for flight and encouraging Larus to do the same.

'No,' demanded Rufus, quickly realising he would be alone. 'I need you,' he expressed, feeling vulnerable at the thought of them leaving. 'I..,I need you both. Without your stories of what happened, Commander Bewick may never believe me on my own.'

'You're a Robin Leader,' Larus said pointing out the obvious, 'are you telling me that they won't believe the bossiest bird in the garden?'

'I am,' he hesitated, pushing his red chest out to emit confidence. 'Proving myself as a Robin Leader, is exactly what I'm doing.'

Larus was quick to react, stretching his white wings as he pondered carefully.

'So, the Commander hasn't officially made you a Garden Leader? Oh dear, now look at you, miles away from your garden. What will the Commander say to that I wonder?'

Defensively, Rufus snapped back, flickering his black eyes at Larus in anger.

'When he hears that I was trapped, he'll understand. Come on, Corax has killed hundreds, probably nearly wiping out our species in the north. The Commander must know. I mean, what if I don't make it there on my own and he never finds out? Could you both live with that?' he expressed, looking at Jack's sullen face and watching Larus as he fidgeted awkwardly.

'Ok, don't do it for me, but do it for those who are about to lose their lives. We know the black sea is coming and they don't,' Rufus shouted, instantly thinking of the danger that Skyla might be in.

Larus and Jack looked at each other, clearly both feeling they had little choice in the matter.

'I suppose, we should make sure he gets there in one piece and doesn't get into a fight on the way,' suggested Jack as he watched Rufus lose his patience and fly off, clearly hoping he would be followed.

CHAPTER 13

NO-ONE HOME

Racing to catch up, Larus and Jack watched Rufus accelerate ahead, as his excitement rose at finally being so close to his home.

'Nearly there, this is it. Watch out for the Squashers though,' he called back, pointing at the cars, which were carefully navigating the flooded roads.

'Oh, and keep your head down, the Beings are everywhere around these parts.'

'Hey, wait for us then,' shouted Larus lolloping behind, realising Rufus's speed was now adrenalin fuelled.

After a while of flying across muddy fields, following broken hedgerows and tumbling walls, Larus and Jack were becoming increasingly tired of hearing Rufus's voice shout, "Watch out this field stinks. Left, right, come on keep up!"

Finally, they approached a gathering of Beings' boxes, as they flew between their walls and over a road. Coming swiftly to perch on a damp cold signpost in the centre of the cu-de-sac which read, '42 Barton Gardens,' under the cover of a large old Pine tree.

Rufus proudly fluffed his feathers and puffed out his chest the excitement at finally arriving home alive rippled through him.

'I'm home,' he said, as he flew off around the sides of a Being's box, entering his back garden, closely followed by Larus and Jack.

'I'm back, hello everyone. I'm alive, I'm here, everything will be ok now. Skyla, where are you?' rattled Rufus's voice through the garden in front of him as he held his head high and waited for the rapturous applause that would surely come.

'I have urgent news…quickly gather around, you lazy lot,' he proudly announced, hoping to see Skyla at any moment.

Rufus was so out of breath it took him a moment to realise that there had been no reply just an eerie silence. Panic began to rise up through Rufus's tiny body, as he began to wonder where on earth everyone was.

Rufus puffed out his chest and in his most instructive voice began… 'This is your Leader speaking. I command your attendance at once. Skyla, Skyla!' Hoping that it would work, he scanned the bare looking hedgerows for any sign of life.

Over and over again he called, his eyes frantically scanning his territory.

Larus, who had been observing the lack of birds, started searching for food as he said, 'Well, not much of a welcome, are you sure this is your territory? Where is your feisty lady friend?'

Ignoring him, Rufus didn't stop flying as he went from hedgerow to bush, using his beak to look under every last crispy brown leaf for hidden birds.

'Jack, help me. They are all here somewhere,' he shouted.

Yet having surveyed the garden territory himself, Jack quickly realised what Rufus was about to experience.

'Come on, Rufus, there's no one here,' he said, clearly knowing the importance of a Robin's Community.

'But I don't understand, what's happened…where is everyone? I should never have left. What will the Commander think? Skyla, where are you?' cried Rufus out loud.

'Who is Skyla?' asked Jack gently.

'She's my partner, obviously,' snapped Rufus and taking a moment to consider, 'well, I was sort of hoping she might be.'

Larus suddenly perked up, 'sort of hoping? So, she not officially Mrs Rufus then?

'Not now Larus,' snapped Jack, as he turned his attention to Rufus and tried to reason. 'All right then, steady on. Look, there's no-one here. We'll find them but…,'

'But?' snapped Rufus, 'but what? You think they would leave without me? No way, Jack, you are wrong!'

Suddenly something caught Jack's eye in the sky above as two black silhouettes flickered in front of the sun.

'Rooks, did you see them?'

Rufus quickly looked up as the two birds took flight from the tops of their huge Pine tree, heading straight for them.

'Oh no, not now. They're the last thing we need,' Rufus snarled.

Larus quickly stopped looking for any misplaced food and began to look uncomfortable. 'Oh, gotta go, you two will be just fine from here I'm sure.'

Rufus turned to see the worry in Larus's eyes, 'You have to, what?'

'Go, I have to go. Good luck. Lovely to meet you both,' he called as he disappeared off across the tops of a nearby woodland.

'Larus, No! We need you, don't go,' replied Rufus in disappointment.

Jack on the other hand did not look quite so surprised at Larus's reaction.

'Let him go, Rufus, you can never trust Seagulls anyway.'

'But he saved us? Why wouldn't I trust him?' questioned Rufus.

'I was told never to trust them,' Jack said, 'and this lot as well.' he added, as they both watched two sniggering Rooks land in front of them.

'Well, welcome home, Rufus. Lost your Community, have you? How forgetful of you,' teased one of the two Rooks, swaggering as he approached Rufus and then standing confrontationally with his skinny black legs apart.

Rufus, did not have time for this nonsense. In all his short, yet busy life, he had lived under the scrutiny of these Rooks, monitoring his every move and always there ready to charge him with one violation or another.

'Where is everyone?' Rufus demanded, looking the Rook in the face with his tiny black eyes. The Rook's large strong grey beak and his piercing expression had never worried him and he wasn't about to let it now.

'I think the question is, 'where have you been, young fella?' questioned the Rook insincerely.

'Fighting for his life, against the black sea that you caused!' shouted Jack, surprising himself as well as Rufus who was standing nearby.

'Oh, careful with those accusations, little one. Fighting for your life… eh Rufus? And clearly making the oddest friends whilst doing so?' said the Rook cleverly, having noticed Larus disappearing off in the grey skies above a few seconds earlier.

'He's right, though isn't he? Corax's evil has nearly wiped us out around these parts, Lord Morus will never let him get away with this,' Rufus said, starting to lose his patience with the Rook who was now pacing around in front of him. 'Now, where is my Community?'

'Really, you two need to be careful who you accuse,' the Rook said slowly. 'Anyway, you weren't here, you were off discovering the world. Didn't your parents ever say that you mustn't leave your territory? Oh, what would they think of you now, Rufus? Looking down upon their son?' he sniggered, enjoying winding up the young snarling Robin in front of him.

'Don't bring my parents into this. Their blood is on your claws. You are evil, pure evil!' Rufus spurted out, feeling his emotions overflowing.

'Oh, steady now, you're making me quake with fear,' laughed the Rook.

'Where have you taken them?' demanded Jack, realising that Rufus looked far too angry to even speak.

The Rook looked mischievously at Jack.

'They have been evacuated by the Starlings if you must know. And, as you mention my Lordship Corax, I am delighted to inform you that the very land you stand on is now finally under his control. You are, in effect, trespassing.'

Rufus's heart nearly stopped at the Rook's words. 'Trespassing? Never! This land will always be Lord Morus's and my territory on his behalf. Again, I shall ask this only once more, where did they take them?' Rufus trembled in anger.

'Don't worry, your lady friend led them away,' added the Rook, eager to see Rufus' reaction.

'My lady friend?' questioned Rufus, and then quickly realised what he meant, 'Skyla? Skyla was here?' he said, as it fully dawned on him what she would have gone through.

'Oh, that's her name, feisty that one, Rufus, I'd be careful if I were you,' chuckled the Rook. 'Anyway, they headed towards the Northern Station, as that's the only land which Commander Bewick actually rules for Lord Morus anymore,' he chuckled. 'So, it's my pleasure to give you the choice of leaving immediately or being 'dispatched'?

Rufus could feel his insides fizzing, luckily Jack had also noticed and was tugging at his wings.

'Come on, Rufus, we need to leave now.' Jack said.

'This is my territory, always was, always will be,' demanded Rufus, his eyes almost exploding in rage, 'and don't think for a moment that I will ever forget…'

'Forget what?' interrupted the Rook.

'This was my parent's rightful territory and…I shall

avenge their deaths...,' expressed Rufus, feeling every instinctive bone in his body telling him to stay and fight.

'Oh, there you go again, Robin, making me shake...oh, I'm so scared,' replied the Rook slowly and sarcastically.

'It is not worth it, Rufus, come on, don't do this today. Remember the Black Sea? Come on, we have no time to lose,' Jack urged, hoping he could pull Rufus away.

'I think your Sparrow friend wishes you to go, Rufus,' sniggered the Rook.

Unexpectedly, the back door swung open on the Being's House as several young looking, noisy Being boys ran out into the garden.

Immediately the Rooks took to the skies, croaking, 'Good riddance,' as they turned their necks to watch Jack taking his chance to drag Rufus away over the hedgerows.

Chapter 14

REGULUS

As the winds increased their strength, it took all the energy the two tiny Songbirds had just to keep to the route ahead. Each layer of wind they encountered, each twist and turn strained against their wings.

Jack was clearly hoping that conversation would break the monotony, so flew up close to Rufus.

'Phew, slow down Rufus, this is killing me,' Jack puffed.

'It is hardly killing you. Come on, faster,' Rufus shouted back, trying to hide his tired expression.

'Talking of killing, is it true then? Was Corax to blame for your parents' deaths?' Jack asked, taking Rufus by surprise.

'What kind of question is that at a time like this? Yes, of course it is true,' Rufus snapped back, closing his eyes as if trying to block out the memory. 'I really don't want to talk about it, Jack.'

As Rufus turned to look at Jack, he had slowed down, appearing to leave space between them, which was the last thing he wanted.

'Come on, faster Jack, we have to make it to the Commander before nightfall, he must know what has happened. And goodness knows what Skyla must think of me now? I really need to talk to her and check she is safe,' Rufus called back, hoping to distract anymore questions, as the gloomy darkening landscape whizzed by below them. 'I am pretty certain if we keep flying in this direction, we should make it.'

'Pretty certain?' questioned Jack. 'I'd rather you were totally certain if I'm honest. If not, we are likely to starve to death…again,' he added, sarcastically.

'What do you suggest I do, stop and ask for directions?' snapped Rufus, clearly feeling it was beneath him to do such a thing.

'That's the best idea you have had all day,' shouted Jack, surprising Rufus, 'and I know just the fella to help, I'm sure he lives around here somewhere, follow me,' he called taking a direct dive for the ground.

'What the heck are you doing, Jack, we will run out of light?' called Rufus, angry that Jack had taken charge and was heading off in another direction. 'Who are you looking for anyway he asked?' watching Jack land and then immediately begin searching under a nearby bush.

'You'll see,' answered Jack confidently, 'anyway, I thought you Robins loved being under bushes?'

'We do, but not right now. Jack, the light is fading. Will you stop messing around.' Rufus said, landing beside him and flapping his wings around to make his point.

Quickly spotting something up ahead, Jack called, 'Come on,' as they flew alongside the angriest looking river they had ever seen.

Chocolate brown, the sheer force of the fumy water was battling its own riverbanks, sending huge lumps of dirt floating past them.

'Stay back,' cautioned Jack, noticing Rufus getting a bit too close, 'I know it's probably the only river you've ever seen but it's probably poisonous,' gently insinuating that Rufus had never left his own garden territory.

Rufus threw Jack an angry look, as they landed on the low branches of an old silver birch tree, which was battling the winds itself.

Noticing Jack was still eagerly looking around, Rufus asked again, 'Who are you looking for? No bird in their right minds would be out here now? Goodness knows why we are?'

'You'll see,' Jack repeated, ignoring Rufus's impatience.

After a few seconds they started to become aware of the feeling of being watched. Swinging their heads around quickly, they noticed a brightly coloured bird peering at them from the branch above.

'Regulus,' shouted Jack.

Covered in feathers of sparkling electric blue and emerald green, the birds head appeared slightly squashed into his shoulders, hunched on his perch. His black eyes oozed wisdom, and yet, there was as air of sadness about him.

'Are you a…Kingfisher?' stuttered Rufus abruptly.

'Yes, clearly,' answered the Kingfisher wisely, looking at the Robin with an expression that suggested he had met many Robins in his long life and knew exactly what to expect. Turning to Jack he said in a soft voice, 'Jack, it's good to see you're alive.'

'How are you? It's been a while,' replied Jack, clearly happy to see an old friend.

'Indeed, it has.' Regulus answered.

'And your partner?' Jack asked.

Regulus lowered his head, 'I lost her, last winter. These are grave times, Jack, it is likely I'm one of the last left.'

'What? No? I am so sorry,' Jack replied awkwardly, not knowing what to say.

'What are you two doing out here anyway?' Regulus said, eyeing up the state of Rufus's ruffled wings and the look of impatience he wore.

'I'm Rufus, Leader of 42 Barton Gardens, Little Hopping, just so you know,' Rufus interrupted proudly, wondering how on earth Jack knew such a rare bird.

Regulus nodded thoughtfully.

'Yes, Rufus, I've heard your name before,' he said, causing Rufus to wonder how.

Then turning to look at the skies the Kingfisher carried on, 'Such young, tiny creatures to be out here in the wilds though, what can I do for you?'

Jack hopped up onto the same branch as Regulus, clinging as hard as he could against the wind.

'We need to fly to the Northern Station, inform the Commander that the evil Corax has struck again, causing a deadly black sea. If we follow this river are we sure to reach it?' he garbled quickly.

'Corax turned the sea black? Surely such atrocities are beyond even him? You must be careful who you accuse in these dangerous times,' Regulus cautioned, overlooking Jack's actual request.

'Oh, of course it was him. Who else would have caused such a mess?' corrected Rufus from below, sensing that this Kingfisher was about to lecture him, as most older birds did.

'Rufus, listen to me and listen carefully. For sure, Corax wishes to take over these lands from Lord Morus's reign. But creating a deadly black sea to clear the lands and ocean for his own Army's use? No, it is just not possible. I'm afraid, its creator is far more sinister.'

'You're wrong, it's him alright,' urged Rufus, unable to concede any other explanation and not really listening to him.

Jack, on the other hand, was watching Regulus carefully. 'What do mean, 'more sinister'? How could the situation be more sinister?'

Regulus eagerly started looking around him for any birds that might overhear him. Satisfied they were alone, he looked again at the two tiny birds.

'It is not really for me to say…,' he hesitated, much to the annoyance of Rufus.

'Say what?' Rufus snapped, flapping his wings and fluffing his red chest to keep warm as he realised this was going to take longer than he originally thought.

'Well, you see, for years there have been rumours that

lands across the Southern Hemisphere have been lost entirely, their weather furiously hot. They say it's heading this way and if that's true we are in far more trouble than we think. It's almost as if Mother Nature herself is destroying her own planet, rather like she did centuries ago when Dinosaurs walked this earth.'

'Dinosaurs?' questioned Jack with interest, becoming increasingly uncomfortable with Rufus's rudeness.

'They were the largest creatures that ever lived, far mightier than the Beings. Legend has it that over the centuries, they began to disrespect each other in such a way that it angered the very spirit of Mother Nature herself. Her anger grew so strong at their contempt for each other that she ended up destroying them entirely, as if she had made a mistake in designing the species in the first place.'

He paused with concern and then noticing Rufus's impatience quickly carried on, 'Yet, we survived only because we could fly and get out of the way of her volcanoes, floods and earthquakes and the balls of fire flying through the skies. So, when the Beings came along, we vowed to respect each other so we could all live in the harmony, it was our 'Sacred Agreement. We would help spread the flowers, plants and trees, allowing them to produce their food. They would feed us and offer us nesting spaces in return.'

Rufus's patience ran out, as he interrupted, 'And, so, what has all this got to do with Corax?'

Choosing to ignore him, Regulus carried on, 'Of course, under the guidance of the Great Lord Morus and generations of his family, we have lived side by side with the Beings for centuries. Rumours are going around that

Mother Nature is angry once again, but this time with the …Beings. It is said that she believes they have destroyed these lands and Corax is merely making the most of the situation for his own gains.'

'Rubbish,' shouted Rufus, 'how could you ever say such a thing? Corax is behind all of this and I am going to help stop him.'

Regulus turned his wise head towards Rufus and gently suggested.

'If it's true and the Beings are behind this, we don't want to be anywhere near her when she ultimately decides to wipe them out, starting from the Southern Hemisphere and working her way North,' he exclaimed.

Quickly retaliating, Rufus spurted out, 'Yes, well then. Good job the Beings haven't destroyed the planet, as why would they? Come on, we gotta get out of here and fast.'

Jack looked surprised at Rufus' rudeness.

Regulus watched Rufus thoughtfully, pushing his large orange chest out and flicking his blue tail feathers.

'My advice, if you will listen, is to look and think carefully about what you see in front of you. Do not be driven by your feelings.'

'Feelings? I haven't time for feelings.'

Regulus nodded knowingly and carried on. 'I hope I'm wrong about the Beings, but either way you're right about Corax's Army as it remains strong. They are clearing these lands of Morus's communities and will think nothing of killing anyone who gets in their way.'

'We'll take our chances,' confirmed Rufus, never having been one for storytelling, as he fluffed up his wings ready for flight. 'Come on, Jack. I need to reach Skyla. Let's catch the next gust of wind, here it comes....'

Jack quickly turned to Regulus realising his time had run out. 'Take care of yourself, Regulus, move whoever you can to safer grounds. And, I am sorry about Rufus. He is right about one thing though; the black sea is coming your way.'

Regulus nodded slowly, clearly having met Robins like Rufus before. Pointing his wing to the south he said. 'You're right to follow the river, go as fast as you can and be careful. Good luck, Jack.'

Testing the direction of the wind, both birds leaped up and allowed the strong gusts to blow them, speeding through the air and managing to follow the fierce brown gushing river below them, as it snaked its way across the landscape.

Flying as close as they could, they watched as the sun began to fade, causing a feeling of urgency rise inside of them.

'Come on, Jack, keep up, we're running out of time,' shouted Rufus, as they both battled the chilly winds.

Suddenly, out of the corner of his eye, Jack spotted shapes flying straight towards them through the icy rain. 'Look, Rufus, over there.'

'Watch out Jack, it is the Nightshift, they are not going to be happy with us,' Rufus replied.

Flying in a long line, several beautiful white Barn Owls were quickly leading a host of other species across the darkening skies, each wearing a look of panic on their faces.

As the leading Owl got closer he shouted across the skies.

'What are you two doing out here? It is far too dangerous, come on, we need to get everyone to the Station before the night truly sets in.'

Flapping their wings as hard as they could, they only just managed to join the main flock as they flew by.

'Surely, so many birds are a violation of Mother Nature's rules? What if the Beings see us all together?' shouted Jack at one of the Ducks who was flapping madly beside them to keep up.

'We had no choice, an urgent meeting has been called for tonight's Chamber by Commander Bewick himself, and we are the last to be gathered up. Now, fly close to me, I'll try and protect you both from the winds.'

Seconds later the entire flock were distant dots on the horizon, as rain started to fall, feeding the angry brown river below.

CHAPTER 15

THE CHAMBER

Rufus watched in awe, as the Owls ahead of him in the sky battled to guide the unusual flock through the stormy clouds, keeping everyone together as best they could.

After several miles, the exhaustion started to show on the faces of the flock, as they felt relieved to spot the glimmering waters of the lakeside Northern Station below.

'Join this gust, let it carry us all,' shouted one of the Owls from the front, as the entire flock visibly relaxed to let the wind take them down to earth.

Jack took a moment of freefall to get Rufus's attention, clearly relaxing his tired wings as he did so, 'What did you think to Regulus's legend?'

'I've never heard of the "Dinosaurs", whoever they were?

No, I mean, why would the Beings destroy the place they live in, it doesn't make sense,' replied Rufus, also enjoying letting gravity take the strain, 'anyway, how do you know him?'

'I was born close to his river; my parents knew him. Don't underestimate him, he's one of the most knowledgeable birds I know. He wouldn't lie,' confirmed Jack, noticing Rufus' attention span had already expired.

Slowly, the flock began to lose height, aiming for the grassy reedbeds next to a wooden Chamber by the water itself.

One of the brown Tawny Owls at the front started to survey the space below, 'Keep to the left, steady as we go and remember, silence as we land.'

Eventually, every bird was pleased to feel the earth under their feet as they gently landed. On hearing them arrive, the ground crew quickly swung into action. Swiftly, several Dragonflies used their reflective blue bodies to guide each bird to gather outside the Chamber.

'Wait here,' they called, pointing with their bony legs, 'remain together at all times and silence please, we must respect the night time rules.'

Feeling constrained, Rufus eagerly started scanning the area for any signs of Skyla.

'Jack, I need to find her, she should be here somewhere,' he whispered eagerly, looking like he was about to fly off.

'Shhhh…, probably now is not the time, stay here,' Jack sternly whispered, watching the Tawny Owl next to them scowl, who was then accosted by one of the Dragonflies.

'We have been waiting for ages,' the Dragonfly said,

'where have you been? It is freezing out here for us. Anyway, the Chamber is ready to sit, come on.'

The Tawny Owl's exasperated expression let the fluttering Dragonfly know that it had gone too far, and was potentially looking quite tasty to the Owl, causing the insect to change the subject.

'Arrh, now if you'll follow me…kindly, please,' said the Dragonfly, flying off towards the Chamber.

In haste, the line of birds hopped up onto the wooden plank and began approaching the large oak doors of the Chamber itself, where two huge dark green warty Toads guarded the entrance.

'Password,' they bellowed, as one caught an unsuspecting dozy fly with their unusually large tongue.

'Out of hibernation as well I see? Well, you know who I am, now open the doors will you?' asked the Dragonfly.

'Password,' repeated the Toads, unmoved by the comments and dedicated to their duties.

'Oh, all right. The password is "Beings,"' snapped the Dragonfly as the Toads nodded and slowly moved the Chamber's doors, as they creaked open.

Immediately, an extremely strong smell of fish and stagnant water filled Rufus and Jack's nostrils as they hopped inside. As their eyes became accustomed to the dim light, it was the sheer sight of what they saw which took some time to comprehend.

From the outside the Chamber had appeared small and yet inside the space was as large as a Cathedral. Rufus looked above him and noticed each wall was stacked to the ceiling with rows of wooden shelves laden with birds, all lined up in their species groups. From the tops of Chamber where the Regiments of Starlings perched, to the middle shelves which was full of garden Songbirds from Blue Tits to Blackbirds and highly painted Goldfinches, all chattering to themselves. One Blackbird in particular, caught Rufus's eye, as he noticed that it looked to be working its way along the middle ledge, getting in everyone's way as he chatted eagerly to each bird, clearly annoying some of the Ducks and Geese perched below. 'Was that Merula?' thought Rufus, watching the Black Moorhens with their orange beaks snarl at the Blackbird, as he used their heads as stepping stones to move along the Chambers ledges. Reaching the end of the line, the Blackbird stopped abruptly, as he came across the large light brown heads of the Greylag Geese who hissed angrily at him, shouting. 'We don't care about your stories Merula, now is not the time!'

Colourful, noisy and with feathers flying in all directions the Chamber buzzed with energy. Every bird's gaze was centred on Commander Bewick and his beautiful partner in the centre of the Chamber, lit only by the light of the moon coming through a small slit in the wooden panelled side of the building.

Jack tugged at Rufus's wing, 'Come on, lets perch down here,' he said, dragging Rufus into the last dark corner of space.

'Jack, maybe Skyla is in here? Look out for her, will you?' Rufus ordered in a low voice, as he continued to scan the Chamber for signs of her.

'I've never met her, Rufus, how I am supposed to know what she looks like?' replied Jack.

'A female Robin? You know, red chest, bossy?' replied Rufus in a matter of fact way.

'Oh, well that's helpful of you,' Jack teased back, quickly noticing Rufus's attention had been taken again.

'How am I going to get the Commander's attention now?' Rufus questioned.

'Shhhhh,' A long line of black Moorhens with red beaks warned behind him, silencing them both.

Together, they watched several white Owls enter gracefully through holes in the roof and perch. The Dragonflies criss-crossed around the inside walls of the Chamber, trying to keep order and encourage silence so that an impatient looking Commander Bewick could begin.

After a few seconds they noticed the large Swan whispering to one of the smallest brown birds in the Chamber.

Hopping forward, the brown Wren gulped, pushed out her brown speckled chest, opened her beak and shouted at the top of her voice.

'Silence. This Chamber is sitting. All quiet please.'

Immediately, the whole Chamber fell silent, clearly surprised by the strength of the Wren's voice from such a tiny body.

'Why must it take a Wren to silence you all? I need order in my Chamber,' demanded Commander Bewick, scanning the room as if trying to make eye contact with every bird within in it.

'We are in session and I will not be interrupted,' he continued, 'tonight, you have been invited to this emergency meeting because we have never faced such destructive times, threatening our very existence and the lands we call home.'

His curt tones bounced off the chamber's wooden walls, as every bird started to listen intently.

'Corax's Army has struck again and this time in a manner so deadly it is beyond belief. Hundreds have died at the destructive path of his black sea and our coastal territories destroyed overnight. As I look around this Chamber, we could be the only remaining birds left in this Northern part of Lord Morus's lands,' he sighed, turning to the white Owls. 'Canopus, Alba, we owe it to you both that we have safely gathered here tonight, thank you.'

The Owls slowly nodded to acknowledge him, as the Commander carried on.

'We all know Corax's grasp of our lands strengthens by the day. His Army patrols every perching structure across this Northern Territory, intimidating each and every one of our communities that are left,' he bowed his head sombrely. 'With no sign of the spring to nourish us, and Corax's threats are so evil, it is a battle to simply…live. So, it saddens me to inform you, that I shall be urgently asking Lord Morus himself to send us reinforcements from the south. Never, across the generations of my family, have we asked his Lordship to help but I fear without it, we risk too many lives being lost.'

A gasp rattled through the Chamber at the Commander's words.

Captain Mallard quickly announced, 'Sir, we will set off at daybreak for Lord Morus's sacred seat of Andromeda, with not a moment to lose. I am sure his Lordship will know what to do.'

Out of the darkness a frightened new voice broke the moment, 'Corax didn't create the black sea, the Beings did.'

Commander Bewick quickly swung his head in the direction of where the voice had come from, closely followed by everyone else, 'What do you mean?' he shouted sternly as other voices began to shout up…

'No, the blackness has been created by Mother Nature's anger, she is finally cracking and our time is running out.'

'Now, hang on a moment,' said the Commander trying to take back control.

'Are you crazy? Of course, it is Corax. Mother Nature would never destroy her own soils and pollute the very water we drink, you crazy fool,' another voice from the other side of the Chamber called.

'Everyone, calm down…' Shouted the Commander, beginning to feel the atmosphere intensifying.

'That slime is not capable of such black magic, it is the Beings, they have destroyed our lands and stirred Mother Nature's anger. This is the end I tell you!' Voices sounded, gaining momentum.

'No, no…,' Rufus started to mutter to himself, as he and Jack watched in horror as Captain Mallard and the Dragonflies tried to bring the Chamber back under control.

Yet, it was the mighty voice of the Wren again that eventually brought order to the room, as Commander Bewick flapped his huge wings and stepped centrally into the shaft of moonlight.

'Order! Order,' he shouted, doing his best to exert his

presence across the Chamber, 'with the help of Lord Morus we will find the truth, somehow,' he said sternly, looking across his audience before announcing: 'It is, I agree difficult to believe that Corax is capable of creating such evil but at this moment, the evidence points to him. You must all remember that we hold a sacred agreement with the Beings themselves. We have been loyal to them for centuries. So, I find it difficult to believe that they would wish to destroy their own planet, or risk losing our respect and the fact that we help grow their food,'

He flapped his wings with a need to change the subject. 'From today, we stick together to discover the truth, fight to defend our freedoms of this vast Northern Territory and remember everything we do is in his Lordship's name.' He raised his wings a second time and shouted, 'here's to Lord Morus!'

His words were quickly chanted throughout the whole Chamber, until a voice shouted again from the darkness.

'What happens when the black sea arrives here, Sir?' Silence descended upon the Chamber once again.

'Captain Mallard and my Starling Regiment will do everything they can to defend our important stronghold from such poison, you have my assurance on that. Yet, each and every one of you must be prepared; be alert to danger. For now, we are not sure if it will even reach us, or exactly how far away it is. Isn't that right, Captain?' the Commander asked as his Captain nodded in agreement.

Rufus and Jack, who had been eagerly listening to every word, looked at each other knowingly, and then quickly to the Barn Owls who were now nodding off to sleep beside them, recovering from their flights.

'Do you think they are going to say anything?' whispered Jack to Rufus, 'this is surely their moment, as we saw how far away it was when we flew in earlier.'

'I don't think they are going to move, come on, Jack,' said Rufus, beginning to move through the crowd in front of them.

'No, wait, Rufus, this isn't the right time,' Jack preached, trying to stop him.

'Commander Bewick, I know how far away the black sea is,' he shouted, pushing his red chest out to make him appear larger than he actually was.

'Who calls my name?' said Commander Bewick, as his gaze urgently went around the Chamber and finally landed on the small rough looking young Robin in the corner, 'Rufus, is that you?'

'Yes Sir,' Rufus said proudly to a chorus of gasps from around the Chamber.

'You're alive, Rufus?' expressed Commander Bewick, clearly relieved.

Rufus wasted no time as he launched into his update, forgetting to look up at the Commander's face, which was now seething.

'Well, the black sea is heading straight for the Station, we flew over it on the way here tonight, it's about five hedgerows away I would think,' he reeled off, as Jack stood by his side, looking embarrassed at Rufus's abrupt attitude.

'So, you left your garden territory unattended in this time of crisis? Why? For what? You have a responsibility,

Rufus. What would your father, Rubecula, have to say?' The Commander boomed angrily, surprising the entire Chamber and cutting through Rufus's dignity like lightening, leaving him speechless.

'Nothing to say Robin? True Robin Knights never leave their post' the Commander said, as he turned to look into the eyes of his disapproving partner beside him. 'I suppose you have survived the greatest loss; that of your parents. But, why would you leave your post, Rufus?'

Doing his best to pull himself together, Rufus shook his wings with all the importance he could muster, as every bird stared eagerly at him.

'I was searching, Sir, searching for food and a better place for my Community to live. Yet all I found was death.' Rufus explained, trying to hold back the emotion he felt.

The Commander paused for a moment, looking deep into the eyes of the frightened young Robin in front of him.

'Your father was one of the finest Robin Knight's I have ever met, he always had a way of living on the edge. He will not be forgotten. But Rufus, we live in far more dangerous times than your father did and you must be responsible. Do you understand me? How can I trust you again?'

Rufus nodded and began fluffing out his small red chest awkwardly, hoping it would give him some confidence. 'Sir, you can trust me. My Community is my home, I will do anything to fight and defend it. You have my word.'

Hoping the conversation would change, Rufus watched as the Commander stayed intently focused on him, without speaking and clearly deep in thought.

'How fast was the blackness travelling?' the Captain

eventually said.

'Oh, quite quick. It was tricky to tell,' replied Rufus urgently, hoping he was saying the right thing. 'But it really isn't that far away.'

As his words rang through the Chamber, chaos erupted, causing feathers to fly in all directions. The unrest almost made the wooden walls wobble from side to side. It took the might of the tiny Wren's voice, whose voice had a distinct croak under the continual pressure, to once again silence everyone.

The strain was clearly showing on the once elegant face of Commander Bewick, 'Are you sure, Rufus, of what you saw?'

'Yes Sir, I mean, maybe we have until the morning? It is hard to say,' Rufus said, realising the impact of his words and worrying that the Commander may never trust him again.

Taking in a deep breath, Commander Bewick looked to the roof of the Chamber for inspiration, as if the answer might be there. Then, slowly he turned to look at his beautiful wife, her elegant white neck and kind eyes told him what he needed to know. Watching the tears begin to steam down her face, as he lowered his head for a few seconds, before looking down upon Rufus once again. 'I know, that what you have experienced, no Robin or any species of bird should have encountered. But I must still be able to trust you, Rufus,'

'Yes, Sir. I know Sir. But..,' Rufus said, trying to be as respectful as he could, yet their remained only one thought in his mind...

'But what?' The Commander asked.

'Have you seen my Community? Have you seen Skyla the Robin?' Rufus asked, hoping he would just answer his only question.

Captain Mallard waddled forward, 'Skyla is here, everyone is safe within the Station,'

'Thank you,' Rufus replied clearly relieved, as he felt Jack tugging at his wing to pull him away.

The Commander sighed and turned to Captain Mallard, 'The dawn is not far away, it gives us no time. Corax's Army will be gathering around us for sure, just as the black sea threatens our very existence. Command the regiments to keep watch through the night. This Chamber is finally dismissed.'

'Come on, Jack,' shouted Rufus eagerly realising they had an opportunity to escape the embarrassment, 'I have to get out of here. Anyway, we need to find Skyla before Corax gets here.'

Wasting no time, the two tiny birds squeezed their way out of the packed Chamber and finally hopped into the cool air of the night.

Chapter 16

Moving Out

In the early hours of the next day, the sun was searching for an opportunity to break through the clouds above an old railway viaduct, a mile away from the Northern Station. Perched proudly along the tops of its walls, Corax's Army stood on guard across the landscape. Their Master commanding a central position in their long line.

'This is our moment, my friends, victory is close by,' Corax sniggered as the dawn's frozen air flowed out of his nostrils like smoke. 'I've dreamt of this very moment, look, the river of poisonous black goo is helpfully about to make its entry into the Station as well. What perfect timing.'

As Corax stretched out his feathers, asserting his authority, the Army watched as the fumy river passed beneath them.

'Shortly, Commander Bewick will have no choice but to evacuate his precious, yet pathetic Community north. Ultimately irretrievably weakening Lord Morus's hold of the Northern Territories. All we will have to do is move in behind them. Oh, the joy of when a plan comes together, it is almost too much to bear,' he gloated, rubbing his wings together in glee.

'Sir, look. Not long now,' confirmed Tobias the Raven, as they all watched a flock of Commander Bewick's Starlings fly past the thick black river, clearly assessing the danger which lay ahead of them.

Gradually, as the polluted air from the river below reached Corax, he announced in excitement.

'Oh, the smell of sweet success, get ready everyone. Wait for my command.'

Back at the Northern Station, the night had passed quickly for Rufus and Jack, who had spent their entire time searching every bush and tree across the northern side of the lake for Skyla. There was only one place left to search but it meant seeking the permission of the Nightshift, and they had been far too busy to even approach.

'She can only be on the south shores of the lake, Jack, we've searched everywhere else. Maybe we just go for it. Come on, we can get across there, who would see?' Rufus said, hunched up on the branch of a bush, taking a moment to rest his aching wings.

'Not the best idea you've had, Rufus. I don't think you need to give the Commander any more reasons not to trust you. Anyway, it is far too dangerous to fly over the lake without help and we can't go around the outside as everyone is strictly in their sections. The Dragonflies would be all over us,' Jack replied, as he wrapped his wings closely around himself to keep out the cold. 'I need to rest anyway, I have a long flight ahead of me.'

'Flight? Where to?' Rufus said, worried that he would be alone.

'You know, to find my own family again. Passer will never forgive me if I don't try and find them and she's not to be messed with, let me tell you. We have delivered the message now, that is all we needed to do together, right?' Jack said.

'Passer?' questioned Rufus.

'My partner, my family. As noisy as they are, I miss them.'

As Jack started to close his eyes, Rufus eagerly replied, 'You have a partner and a family? Why didn't you say?'

'I did, you just don't listen.' Jack said knowingly, watching Rufus attention span predictively disappear.

'I must find Skyla, she must know that I didn't abandon my garden, I was just looking for a better place to live for us and then this goes and happens. Honestly, one day the Commander will understand. He might even give me a mission, just like my father. He was always delivering important missions apparently, how else would he have become the fine Knight he was?'

'Is that all you care about? Being given a mission? Honestly, you Robins never stop. Well, I am sorry to point out the obvious, but you're not exactly the Commanders favourite bird right now, are you?' Jack said, hoping to bring Rufus back into reality.

Rufus appeared to ignore him and carried on. 'Well, you can't leave me now. It is far too dangerous and anyway how would you get home on your own?'

Begrudgingly, Jack started to tell Rufus that House Sparrows were actually excellent at finding their way home and didn't need the help of the Robins at all, when he quickly realised that Rufus's attention had, once again, been taken elsewhere.

Above them, flying out of the morning's cloudy sky, a Squadron of Starlings landed as quickly as they could in front of the Chamber, immediately demanding that the doors were opened.

As soon as they entered, it wasn't long before the booming voice of Commander Bewick could be heard inside, waking every sleeping bird in the vicinity.

'Corax is close?' his voice bellowed in pain, 'and the black waters are approaching? What choice do I have?'

Quickly invigorated by what he had heard, Rufus turned to Jack.

'Come on, something is about to happen,' he said, as they both flew closer.

After a few seconds, the Starlings flew directly from the Chamber's doors, closely followed by several rather stressed-out looking Dragonflies and finally Captain Mallard who stopped in the doorway.

'Go, let everyone know, we have no time left,' he called to his Squadrons of Starlings, 'Corax's Army surrounds us and it is only a matter of time before the black sea reaches our lake. Once you have alerted the Geese, they will be instantly here to evacuate us. They have trained for this moment for generations, they will know what to do.'

* * *

Across the lake and deep within the 'Travellers Quarters', Skyla Robin sat perched high up in a Beech tree overlooking the lake. Her Community huddled in a long line beside her, still exhausted from their flight the night before.

Together, they watched as bright reflective bodies of Dragonflies appeared from the tops of the Chamber and came shooting across the lake towards them.

'Stay calm everyone,' commanded Skyla, watching the urgency of one of the Dragonfly's speeding towards them, although the insect was somewhat out of breath by the time it reached them.

'I am here to tell you to prepare!' It gasped. 'Get ready to be moved this very instant, Corax's Army is about to attack and the black sea is coming. Now listen, the Starlings will reach you first, taking you safely into the skies and within the path of the oncoming Geese. Who, as you know, will not stop flying. So, you must grab hold as they fly by, it is the quickest and safest way? Do you understand?' It paused and then answered its own question, 'ok, good,' and then buzzed off to the next tree down the line.

First to panic was a group of Blue Tits. 'Do WHAT? Grab hold of WHAT? This is crazy, how on earth are we supposed to do that?'

Further down the tree a group of greener larger Songbirds joined in. 'No way, we can't do that,' chanted the Greenfinches, as panic started to ripple throughout occupants of the entire tree.

Skyla agreed, it did sound crazy. She eagerly looked around her for other Robin Leaders, trying to gauge how they might be controlling their own communities. Oddly, Skyla seemed to be the only Robin around, which made her feel instantly vulnerable and left wondering whether all the other Songbirds around would look to her for their Leadership? She closed her eyes for a second, as the painful memory of Rufus flooded her mind. What would he have done, she thought? Unable to answer the question, she opened her eyes and nervously, tried to calm everyone down.

'Look here, listen to me, I'm sure this will be fine. The Geese are trained professionals and at least the clouds will cover us all from the Beings,' she tried to appease, feeling the full weight of responsibility.

Shaking her wings to loosen the weight of the water droplets, which were clinging to her feathers, she hopped up to position herself in the centre of the tree. Stretching her legs and lifting her tail, seemed to renew her confidence.

'Now, listen up,' she shouted at the top of her voice, 'we have a few moments, take only what you can carry and form a line across this branch. Quick now.'

She watched as her line of panic-stricken Songbirds flapped their wings, equally sending droplets of spray everywhere. Quickly, her attention was turned by the noises coming from the long grasses of the Starling Regiments quarters as they took to the skies. Never before had she heard such a sound, the sheer vibration of hundreds of birds coming together in the sky made the feathers on the back of her neck stick up.

Chapter 17

TAKING TO THE SKIES

'Starling Officer 235 reporting for duty, Sir. Having assessed the situation, I can formally confirm that the black sea has entered the waters of this lake.'

The colour started to drain from Captain Mallard's face as he stood inspecting his Regiment outside the Chamber's doors.

'And, Corax's Army surrounds us. We are outnumbered,' added the Officer, in a matter of fact way.

Abruptly, the Chamber's doors flung open as Commander Bewick and his partner slowly waddled down the plank towards the grassy reed beds. Their once elegant white faces now shone with worry as they looked directly at their Captain for the latest update.

'Commander, his Army has us surrounded and the lake

is going to turn black any moment. It is now too dangerous to stay.'

The pain flickered in Commander Bewick's eyes as he scanned the scene in front of him, hoping to find an answer that would allow him to stay.

'Never, in all the generations of my family have we left our posting at this Station. Never!' he repeated sternly.

'Sir, we have no time. You must announce the command,' urged the Captain, 'our regiments in the south will have informed the Geese by now. Cloud cover is good and it is too early for most Beings to even be out at this time of day. We must seize this moment.'

'You have clearly made the decision for me, Captain Mallard,' hissed the Commander, only to look at his partner who was gently shaking her head at his unsympathetic manner towards his Captain.

'You are right though. Even though every bone in my body, every feather on my back, tells me to stay and fight. I know it cannot be.'

The Captain moved closer, 'Commander, we have always served you to the best of our ability but this is beyond our control now. You're right, we must ask Lord Morus for help. The message must be sent urgently… but by who, Sir?'

'What do you mean, who?'

'We must move the entire Station now, I need every last Starling Officer, Pigeon and even the Owls,' the Captain replied.

With the pressure starting to show Commander Bewick demanded, 'Who then? Someone has to make the journey South, Captain?'

Quickly, they both became aware of two small birds

standing behind them, who had clearly been watching and listening to everything.

* * *

Rarely had Rufus ever felt indecisive. He knew that staying alive often relied on making decisions straight away. But as he watched the Commander and the Captain, in their moment of need, he found himself suddenly torn as the thought of Skyla's safety stuck in his mind. Surely, this was a moment to step forward, prove himself as a potential Robin Knight and offer to help? On the other claw, if he remained silent and continued looking for Skyla, he might just stand a chance of proving himself to her and putting his own Community first. Isn't that what his parents would do he thought? Instantly, allowing the painful memory of them to flood through his body again. Or would they? For a second, deep within his own head, he remembered Percy the Pigeon's voice at the time of their death, "Your father understood his duty to this Community, Rufus. But his heart belonged to being a Knight and answering the 'call' of a mission. Don't ever forget that."

Noticing Jack's pensive face beside him, Rufus hopped forward to join the Captain and Commander.

'Rufus,' snapped the Captain, 'whatever you have to say, now is not the time.'

Rufus fluffed his wings up, attempting to ooze confidence as he announced, 'Sir, let me help you. I am fit for flight and Robins never let anyone down.'

Captain Mallard was quick to shoot him a disapproving look, 'Never let anyone down? You left your post. Anyway, why are you still here? You must re-join your own Community,' he urged, as Jack quickly looked relieved and got ready to fly home.

'Sir, I know I let you both down but you have to trust me. I believe it is what my parents would do and I wish to avenge their deaths so please let me help you.'

As the Captain watched Jack quietly hop away, he turned to Rufus, whose tiny black eyes were full of emotion.

'Rufus, thank you. But you are too young. You have proved that.'

'Too young to lose my parents?' he shouted emotionally.

Commander Bewick stepped forward, appearing to recognise the pain.

'Anger will not solve your suffering, my friend. Patience will…but for that, you'll need to be brave.'

'Sir, I am brave. I am brave and ready. Let us take the message south.'

For a moment, the Commander appeared deep in thought, as he watched Jack continue to try and creep away, the power of his stare brought him to an uncomfortable halt.

'Us?' questioned Jack, 'what do you mean 'us'? I have done my part of this mission, you're on your own now. I need to find my family and surely you need to find Skyla, what are you thinking?'

Ignoring him, Rufus boldly carried on in the hope that Jack would come around.

'You can trust us, Sir, we will complete this mission.'

Commander Bewick looked directly at the feisty Robin in front of him. Time was running out.

'I feel your passion, Rufus, but the journey will be fraught with danger. I cannot risk your lives again, it is too dangerous.'

'Sir, we are brave. We have witnessed the black sea, seen hundreds die in front of our very eyes. We are strong flyers, just show us the way,' beamed Rufus, who was now holding onto Jack as he attempted to hop away again.

The Commander looked Rufus up and down. 'You're still in the first year of life? The journey needs skilled flyers.' As he noticed some small fluffy brown feathers at the tips of Rufus's wings.

'I'll have you know, I'm nearly a year old. And we can both fly as strong as any other,' he said confidently. 'I can even translate some of what the Beings say…well most of it.'

Impressed by Rufus's enthusiasm, the Commander turned and looked around him at the sheer size of the chaos that had been created, his desperate eyes finally resting on the Captain.

'Captain, do I have a choice?' he expressed, already knowing the answer by the look on the Captain's face.

Turning to Rufus, he announced slowly, 'Rufus, if you're up to the task, it is your mission. You must take your friend though, travelling together is far safer.'

As quickly as Rufus was nodding, Jack was shaking his head furiously.

'No, Rufus, find someone else, I'm off,' snarled Jack hopping away.

The Commander and Captain watched Jack with concern, as Rufus fluffed up his wings in embarrassment beside them.

'He'll come around, Sir, don't worry about him,' suggested Rufus optimistically.

'You can't travel alone, Rufus,' explained the Commander, clearly worried about the young Songbirds. He turned and boomed, 'Jack wait.'

Jack stopped and turned back. Aware that everyone was now looking at him, as the pressure built.

'Your friend needs you; we need you,' explained the Commander.

'He is not my friend,' snapped Jack, his words cutting through Rufus.

Ignoring his comment, the Commander carried on, 'You're a fine House Sparrow, Jack. For years I have admired your species for their loyalty and intelligence, and whatever has happened between you two, you must put it behind you. Rufus cannot go alone.'

Rufus watched intensely hoping that Jack would make the right decision. After a few moments, the weight of everyone's stares clearly wore Jack down, as he replied bluntly, 'Fine.'

The Commander quickly continued, 'Right, good. However, your mission is only to fly to the Southern Station, that's it. No further, as the journey onto Andromeda, where Lord Morus nests, will be beyond you both. To do this you have my special permission to take the Skyway south, stick with its energy force and you will be fine,' he said, watching the excitement which was now beginning to grow on Rufus's face. 'When you arrive at the Southern Station, find Commander Monty, tell him he needs to ask Morus for reinforcements to be sent north urgently, do you understand?'

'The Skyway Sir?' questioned Rufus, excited at the thought of being allowed to travel this way, as it was way beyond their usual flying height and only reserved for those birds that travelled the world.

'Yes, Rufus. You must be strong though, it won't be easy to join it with your size of wings. Fly hard and straight up,' confirmed Commander Bewick, whose concentration was returning to the chaos around him.

Rufus's small red chest grew with pride as he bowed to accept their challenge, finally knowing he was trusted again. Although still not sure how he would tell Skyla, if he ever found her again.

Jack on the other hand seemed less impressed, 'I can't believe you have made me do this,' Jack grumped as they started to hop away. 'You have signed us up to die, Rufus! How on this earth are we ever going to fly all that way, we are not Starlings you know?'

Just as Rufus started to try and convince Jack that he needed him, the chilling sound of the Geese could be heard across the other side of the lake. As their honks grew it signalled the huge size of the flock approaching. The Commander immediately turned to his Captain, realising the time had arrived.

'Captain, now,' causing the Captain to quickly turn to the line of Officers in front of them, as they waited for their command.

'Murmurate,' he cried at them, knowing they would immediately react to this secret word.

The sight of thousands of Starlings, rapidly rising to the skies was something to behold. The energy and power of the flocks as they rose in unison even appeared to take the Captain's breath away, and his whole body puffed-out with pride. Dividing in the sky with military precision, each flock consisted of about one hundred birds. Independently, they swooped down to their various different areas of the reeds and lakeside banks to gather the wide variety of birds which required their help in getting ready for the Geese.

CHAPTER 18

THE LOST TERRITORY

Across the other side of the lake, Skyla instantly saw what was happening as the Starlings approached shouting, 'Now, fly, fly, fly!'

Desperately, she tried to make sure that every last bird in her flock had been swept up by the Starlings as they passed by. Finally, checking the Oak tree was empty of birds, she was swept up by the Starlings herself.

It took all the energy Skyla had to keep up with the Starlings, continually flying accurately enough to keep within the flock. They headed across the lake, and started to bank to the left so that they would collide straight into the on-coming black and white Geese, when something on the side of the lake caught her eye.

A scruffy-looking young Robin was hopping excitedly next to a tired looking House Sparrow.

'Rufus!' she called out, realising who she was looking at.

Thinking her heart was literally going to break free from her chest, Skyla found herself temporarily forgetting what she was doing and heading straight for him. It took a few seconds for the Starling regiment to realise that they had lost one of their flock, as Skyla put all her strength into performing a straight dive, causing chaos for the thousands of birds and Starlings that were airborne in the area.

'Watch it,' they cried at her, 'you crazy Robin, what are you doing? You'll kill yourself.'

Skyla didn't seem to care as she continually shouted, 'Rufus, Rufus,' hoping that he would hear her above the commotion.

* * *

Below, on the banks of the lake, it was Jack who spotted the female Robin, approaching the ground at speed.

'Rufus, look!' he said pointing up to the sky with his wing, 'do you know that crazy Robin, she's calling you?'

Rufus couldn't believe it, and as the adrenaline instantly sped through his body, he leaped into the air to meet her, 'Skyla, is that you?'

As Skyla began flapping her wings to slow her fall and Rufus accelerated his vertical flight, they embraced mid-air for a split second.

'You're alive Rufus, alive,' Skyla whispered for a spilt second, as an expression of anger started to grow across her face.

Oblivious, Rufus turned to guide them to earth, as

he suddenly felt the weight of Skyla's wing slapping him against his face.

'What was that for!' Rufus retaliated in shock.

'For inviting me to your garden and then leaving me in charge. How could you! Do you know what I've been through?' Skyla shouted against the chaos of the skies around them.

'I know, I am so sorry. Believe me, that's not what I had planned,' Rufus replied emotionally, as they both landed softly together.

'What had you planned? What did you want to tell me?' Skyla asked, mellowing.

Rufus had no time to answer as Starlings and Dragonflies immediately started to surround them. Once the whole Squadron of Starlings had dropped into place the current Officer stepped forward. 'I am Officer 423, the time has come to leave, please follow your Squadron for your own safety,' he shouted above the din of noise around them.

'Yes, of course,' said Skyla, 'come on, Rufus. Your Community needs you and definitely not me. It is such a responsibility looking after that lot isn't it?' she chirped, waiting for a reply, which never came…

'What is it, Rufus?' she questioned, realising he wasn't moving, 'come on, we must go.'

Commander Bewick, who had been watching the scene unfold, lowered his neck towards Skyla and gently announced. 'I have given Rufus a mission, it is vital to our species that he delivers it. You must let him go.'

Skyla immediately looked at Rufus to confirm that surely there had been some mistake, 'Rufus? Is this true?'

'Yes, but I can explain, Sky listen to me,' he said, predicting this wasn't going to be an easy conversation.

'Rufus, you left me once. You wouldn't do it again, would you?' she pleaded, tilting her head as Robins do.

The guilt started to cut through Rufus, as he realised Skyla was right.

'Sky, I can't help it, I have to help. It's what my parents would have wanted me to do,' insisted Rufus.

'And what about what I think? Or don't you care for me, like that?' Skyla shouted. Not offering Rufus any chance to reply, she carried on. 'You invite me to your garden, then abandon it. I had to take on your Community, as apparently, I had no choice, Robin Law and all! Which, I didn't want to do, by the way. Goodness knows what my parents would think if they knew where I was now,' Skyla stropped, turning her head the other way to make her point.

'Skyla, wait. You have to understand. I didn't want any of this to happen but please understand. I have to do this mission, Corax must be stopped. Come on, you're brave, I've seen it in you,' he paused. 'I'll be as quick as I can. Then, when I am home, I'll take charge, giving you everything you need, I promise.' Noticing, as he spoke, the Starlings beginning to close in on Skyla.

'Oh Rufus, you and your missions! No, that's not good enough. I can't do this by myself and I don't see why I should,' screamed Skyla, as she was suddenly grabbed by the Starlings and lifted high into the air, as they headed to join the Geese.

'Sky, be brave! Please take care of my Community, they

need to be protected,' shouted Rufus, as Jack held him back as best he could. 'I'll find you again, I promise,' he called after her.

For a second, Jack watched helplessly as Rufus fought with his instinct to follow Skyla. Then, something caught his eye, high up in the sky.

Flying in one long line, the determined formation of Corax's Army in the sky above caused an immediate sense of panic across the Northern Station. Hundreds of birds took to the skies in a chaotic scene of flapping wings and squeals, which sent feathers flying in all directions.

* * *

Instantly, Commander Bewick stretched out his large white wings. 'What are you all doing! Wait for the Geese, they are coming to take you all to safer grounds,' boomed his curt tones, as Regiments of Starlings Officers flew across the skies trying desperately to assert some order.

Turning to face the oncoming line of Corax's flying Army, the Commander did his best to stand his ground. 'This is Lord Morus's Territory, it will never be yours!'

Flying in the middle of his flock Corax sniggered loudly. 'Oh, we'll see about that, Commander. Looks like you're abandoning these lands, but don't worry, we'll look after them for you.'

'Scavengers,' hissed the Commander.

Overhead, one by one, several Starlings Officers started shouting, 'The black waters, they're here, fly, fly, fly!'

Standing next to the Commander, Captain Mallard,

pushed out his green neck with importance and flapped his wings shouting, 'Now, Sir. The time is now.'

Together, they turned to see the majestic sight of a huge formation of Geese, skimming across the lake's surface at high speed, honking to each other as they flew.

'Get ready, everyone, take to the wing,' the Commander reluctantly boomed, lowering his beak. 'Rufus, Jack, stay here, let them go first.'

A vacuum of pressure appeared to be created, as the sheer weight of the entire flock of birds took to the skies at once. Feathers flew in all directions, as what felt like a million wings flapped for their lives in all directions.

Working hard, the Starlings began cleverly manoeuvring individual flocks of birds, lining them up in mid-air, right within the flying path of the oncoming Geese. Expertly trained, as the Geese flew by several birds were loaded on to their backs. Once secure within their wings, it would take all the strength of the Geese to take their passengers high into the safety of the clouds at speed, honking as they went.

Watching on, the Captain and his Starlings made sure everyone was accounted for. The Commander then turned his final attention to the two tiny songbirds beside him.

'Rufus, Jack, do you see the sun rising over there? Fly as hard as you can towards it, then let the clouds take you due south. As soon as you feel the energy of the Skyway you'll be safe, just follow it. Now go, everyone fly!'

As the fumes from the black waters started to fill their lungs, the decision to follow orders was an easy one. Lifting into the sky, they all turned for one last goodbye. That's when they noticed that Corax's Army had landed a little distance away from the smelly waters of the lake, and surrounded it in such a way that it made clear this territory had been taken.

* * *

'Rufus, where are you going? We need to fly up to the Skyway?' shouted Jack, as he quickly became aware that Rufus had started to fly in the opposite direction.

'I need to make sure Skyla is ok first. I am sure they flew this way,' Rufus shouted back, eagerly searching the ground as it whizzed below them.

Jack reached forward, grabbing Rufus's wing.

'There's no time, we must leave now. You heard what the Commander said.'

'Get off me, Jack! I need to find her and check she is safe first, you heard how angry she was,' Rufus snarled.

It took all Jack's might, as he flew in front of Rufus, stopping him at every turn.

'Will you stop,' he shouted, finally slowing Rufus down. 'You're going to have to trust the Starlings. Come on, Rufus, if you think I want to be here and not finding Passer, you are so wrong. But what choice do I have now, thanks to you?'

Rufus took one last look into the distance behind them. Realising Jack was right, he looked up to the sky. A sinking feeling in his stomach had set in as he questioned himself. Would Skyla and his Community be there when he returned? Would he return? If he was ever going to prove himself a Robin Knight, now was surely that time, 'It is now or never Jack, come on we can do this,' Rufus announced.

Grumbling, Jack agreed. Fluffing their wings together to gather as much air as possible, both birds launched themselves vertically into the air, flying as hard as they could to catch the energy of the Skyway above.

After a few moments, the strain was starting to become unbearable as the two tiny birds tried to pull their bodies up through the darting icy raindrops and against the winds, pushing them back to earth.

'We must be close, Jack, come on,' encouraged Rufus. He began to slowly realise that the air was becoming thick with fog, signalling they had reached the bottom of the clouds.

'That's it, now all we have to do is get above this cloud, I think,' he said turning to look at Jack who was appearing to lose height.

'Hang on,' called Rufus, turning in mid-air, swooping down and grabbing Jack's wing to drag him through the clouds. 'Flap for goodness sake, I can't hold you,' he strained. 'The energy line has got to be here somewhere.'

'No,' shouted Jack in pain, 'the clouds are too wet, Rufus; our wings will get too heavy.'

'Just keep flying up,' Rufus screamed, trying to keep Jack as close to him as possible, knowing that if he let go now they were sure to lose each other within seconds.

From somewhere deep within himself, Jack found the last bit of energy he needed. Flapping his wings, they reached the tops of the clouds and were relieved to eventually feel the magical pull of the Skyway.

'Woo hoo,' cried Rufus instantly, 'this feels awesome!'

He spun in mid-air, carried away with the pure natural

force of the energy line, taking them south and making them feel weightless.

'Amazing,' agreed Jack, 'this is incredible, I've only ever heard of the skyway, never thought I'd actually be allowed to fly in it. Woohoo, the power feels unstoppable.'

Speeding through the clouds with ease gave both birds an opportunity to see Mother Earth below for all she was. Glimpses between the clouds revealed a landscape gripped by the very worst that winter had thrown at it. Slushy fields of mud, large swathes of standing flood waters. Lifeless woodlands and barren hedgerows were dotted about between the massive network of Beings' roads and houses, which appeared to spread across the landscape. Occasionally, any spaces left over were filled high with what appeared to be large mounds of the Beings rubbish, its stench raising high into the skies.

It didn't surprise them that the Northern Station had been under so much pressure, there simply wasn't any space for their species left.

'What are they doing down there do you think?' Jack asked, noticing several long lines of Beings walking together, appearing to hold buckets.

'Not sure, but it looks like they are carrying water to drink maybe? Doesn't surprise me, it is not like they can drink from the rivers. In fact, I wonder, what does clean water taste like?'

'Never had it, I wouldn't know.' Deliberately changing the subject, Rufus called lover, 'Finally though, a mission of my own. It is every Robin's dream, Jack. If only my parents could see me now. If only Skyla would understand,' Rufus allowed himself to imagine for a moment.

'She will Rufus, give her time,' Jack counselled thoughtfully and then asked, 'Was your father really a Knight?'

'He was, one the greatest that ever lived. Or so I am told,' Rufus paused. 'One day, I am going to find out why Corax killed them. There must have been a reason. Finding the truth, will be the only way I will avenge their deaths, even if it's the last thing I do. For now, though, hold tight… Commander Monty here we come!'

THE LAST YEAR OF THE WILD

The adventure series
Set in 2060

Book 1 – Winter

Book 2 – Spring Equinox

Book 3 – Summer Solstice
Release planned for early 2024

Book 4 – Autumn Equinox – 2024

Book 5 – Winter Solstice – 2024

For more information and updates follow:
Website – lizziepepper.co.uk
Instagram- lizzie.pepper1
Facebook- Lizzie Pepper
Twitter- LizziePepper5

To Tom, Lily and Josh
Thank you for putting up with the endless lonely nights, as
I tame the flapping creatures in my imagination. This book
is dedicated with love to you all.

Also to Max, Maisey and Chester, our beloved dogs, for
always looking interested in my stories.

A special thank you must also go to my amazing niece
Grace Moran. Who has helped me bring my characters
alive, through creating these inspirational illustrations.

And finally, thank you to you the reader, as we go on this
adventure together…